The rain was coming down in sheets now, wind driven, and when Venetia reached the covered structure, the sole of her half-boot slipped on the wet stone floor and the result could have been a very nasty fall indeed, had not Nicky been right there to catch her. As it was, the results of this timely intervention were even more disastrous.

For upon finding the delectable Lady Venetia encircled in his arms with her face uplifted toward his in gratitude, Nicky completely lost his head and kissed her. The kiss, despite the water streaming from her bonnet, turned out to be such an agreeable occupation that the thought of terminating it never even occurred to him. . . .

A QUESTION OF CLASS

Marian Devon

FAWCETT CREST • NEW YORK

A Fawcett Crest Book
Published by Ballantine Books
Copyright © 1988 by Marian Pope Rettke

Library of Congress Catalog Card Number: 87-92137

ISBN 0-449-21340-4

Manufactured in the United States of America

First Edition: July 1988

Chapter
One

"**B**ath is no place to mend a broken heart."
Lady Stoke's mouth pursed in unaccustomed disapproval as she looked over the throng collected in the Pump Room. Her situation beside the Tompion Clock offered an ideal vantage point. Just above it, in an alcove, the statue of Beau Nash also watched the crowd, though rather more benignly.

"But I don't have a broken heart, Aunt Louisa." The young lady who shared Lady Stoke's settee was modishly attired in a gray muslin round dress topped by a blue spencer against the cold. She looked at her relative with fond exasperation. "Why do you keep insisting upon a physical impossibility? I've assured you no end of times, that particular organ is perfectly intact."

"Of course your heart's broken. Your engagement was."

This logic was indisputable in the older woman's eyes. Her companion seemed to find it somewhat lacking. But Lady Venetia Lowther managed to bite off the rebuttal that she realized was futile. "I suppose heartbreak is the conventional attitude," she compromised.

"Of course it is. And the only cure for a romance gone sour is to plunge into another as soon as possible. Trust me, Venetia. I'm not entirely without experience in these matters." Lady Stoke's expression caused her niece to think of cats and cream.

"But as I was saying," her ladyship continued after a reminiscing pause, "Bath is the last place on earth your father should have sent you. But then, Lowther never had a brain for anything except politics."

"Father didn't send me," Lady Venetia explained patiently. "As I've told you, Aunt, it was my own idea entirely."

"But you could not possibly have known what Bath is like. You were raised abroad." Lady Stoke contrived to make "abroad" sound like one of the moon craters. "Of course," she added fairly, "I suppose Lowther had no idea himself what Bath's become. It used to be England's most fashionable watering place. But that was eons ago. Now just look around you." A wave of her gloved hand encompassed the full scope of the room, from pump to people. "Every soul here is either an Ancient or an Invalid. Or most likely both. Bath is nothing like it used to be," she said with a sigh, casting her eyes upward toward the statue of Nash, who had presided over the resort in its eighteenth-century heyday when in the eyes of the Beau Monde only London could surpass it in importance. But in 1816, as Lady Stoke was fond of pointing out, the situation was much changed. "You'll find no one but retirees here now, m'dear. Lawyers, doctors, clergymen, half-pay officers. All suffering from some complaint or other that they delude themselves into believing this vile mineral water will cure." She sighed lugubriously, then added in a confidential whisper, "Which, between us, is exactly why I chose to live here. It's a perfect place for a lady in her, er, *middle years* to find male companionship."

Clearly Louisa Stoke did not classify herself as either an Ancient or an Invalid but as the exceptional Bath resident that proved the rule. She admitted to being "fiftyish" but had in truth surpassed her sixtieth birthday the month before. And she could almost get away with it. Her pink silk walking dress and rose-trimmed bonnet of gros de Naples were bravely youthful. She possessed the perfect degree of plumpness to smooth out wrinkles. Her hair defied the laws of nature with dogged goldenness. Her blue eyes were childlike. Her face was amiable.

"Sooner or later, you see," her ladyship continued, "every gentleman of a certain age winds up, glass in hand, over there." She pointed toward the windowed alcove that contained the famous pump. "But this won't do for you, my dear. You really don't wish to wind up marrying some Ancient and fetching his nostrums for him just because your *young* man proved unreliable, now, do you? Trust me. Marrying out of one's generation is no fun at all. I do know whereof I speak, Venetia, for my first husband was a full thirty years my senior. Still," she added fairly, "I can't complain, for he went on to his reward after only ten years of marriage and left me mine—a fortune for my lifetime. But you can't count on being that lucky, Venetia.

3

Besides, I was considerably younger than you, m'dear, when I married Lord Wincanton.

"Anyhow, all that is completely beside the point that I wished to make. My second husband, you see, was only four years older than I, and that marriage was far more satisfactory, if you take my meaning. The point is, the only possible reason to marry an older man, Venetia, is for financial independence. And since you have that already, you should not look for a husband here."

"But I'm not looking for a husband."

"Well, you should be. And London's the proper place to do it. Your aunt Ellis, I'm sure, would be more than happy to—"

"Aunt Louisa," Venetia interrupted her firmly, "please don't start up again. I absolutely refuse to cast myself upon the marriage mart like some chit straight from the schoolroom. The idea's repugnant to me. Not even to mention ludicrous."

"Don't talk fustian. You're not an old maid quite yet."

" 'Quite yet.' See? Even you have me tottering on the brink. Well, I intend to tip right over and accept my single state. There are worse conditions, I assure you, and I'm thankful to have escaped at least one of them."

Lady Stoke opened her mouth to reply but delayed her rebuttal in order to greet a passing dowager weighed down with pearls and weighing down a weary companion by leaning on her arm. Once assured that these acquaintances were out of earshot, her ladyship took up the conversation where they'd left off.

"Being twenty-four years old hardly puts you in your dotage," she said severely. "But one would expect you to be a bit more worldly than a schoolroom miss. If you will forgive my saying so, Venetia, you do seem a bit naive. It comes, I'm sure, from your having lost your dear mother at such an early age. Had you had an older, wiser female to guide you, I'm convinced you never would have broken off your engagement so precipitously. Certainly had I been there to advise you, I should have counseled against any such action. Oh, please don't think me unfeeling, Venetia. I know it must have been upsetting for you to discover that the man you were betrothed to was keeping a mistress. But after the initial shock had worn off a bit, you could have been led to see the advantages to that sort of thing.''

Venetia's expression wavered between amusement and disgust. ''You really are serious, aren't you, Aunt? Personally I should hate to contemplate reaching a stage where I'd be content to share a husband with some—some—lightskirt. Spinsterhood sounds most attractive compared to that.''

Her aunt sighed heavily. ''If you think that, m'dear, you really are deluded. Marriage, any kind of marriage—excepting, of course, to some brute, which in your case has no application—is far superior to a single state. A married woman has all sorts of social latitude denied the spinster. She can do pretty much as she pleases—as long as she's discreet, that is. And it never hurts if her spouse's attention is diverted elsewhere. Providing, of course, that one isn't madly in love with him, which would put an entirely different complexion upon the matter.'' She paused expectantly.

Venetia merely smiled enigmatically and wished her aunt would drop the subject. Had she been in love with Fletcher Langford? She really was not sure. She must have been a little, she supposed. But certainly not madly so.

The young secretary to the British ambassador to Spain had, at the time, seemed the perfect Beau Ideal—handsome, charming, of good family, assured of a brilliant career—especially with her fortune behind him, she added

5

cynically. But when, after a twelve-month betrothal, she had discovered her fiancé's three-year liaison with an opera dancer, it was her pride more than her heart that had suffered, she suspected.

"Perhaps your problem is that you expect too much, my dear," Lady Stoke continued. "Here I've been thinking that your heart surely must be broken, but you assure me that it is not, an attitude that struck me at first as decidedly unromantic. But perhaps your problem is that you are *too* romantic, that, as I said, you expect too much. If so, I lay the blame squarely upon those novels all you young women read nowadays.

"Thank goodness I was never so misguided in my youth. I had no taste for reading at all, I'm glad to say. For no mortal man could ever live up to those impossible heroes who sigh and die for love twenty-four hours out of every day. It's been my experience that gentlemen for the most part—at least after the excitement of pursuit and conquest has worn off—are far more concerned with their dinners and hunts and mills and cards and races—or, if they're of a serious turn of mind, their politics and their estates— than they are with being in love. So it's really foolish of a woman to take the whole thing too seriously.

"Let me put it another way, Venetia. It's all well and good for a woman to be romantic. Why, I've been in love too many times to number and I've certainly no intention of breaking the habit now just because I've reached the age of, er, fifty. But it's when you confuse romance and marriage that the difficulties arise."

"Are you trying to tell me, Aunt, that one should never marry for love?"

"Well, I should not go quite so far as to say 'never.' I was terribly in love with my second husband. And it did make things quite pleasant. For a while, at least. But later, when he was not quite so . . . attentive . . . No, I would not consider that my most successful marriage. There are better reasons for marrying than being in love."

"That, Aunt Louisa, is the most cynical remark I've ever heard you make."

"Cynical?" Lady Stoke mulled the word over and then rejected it. "Certainly not. Worldly, perhaps. I am merely trying to give you good advice, my dear. Above all, a marriage should be comfortable. And for all its appealing qualities love, I can assure you, is seldom that.

"So you really need to adopt a more practical view of life, my dear. All this talk of spinsterhood is foolishness. You must marry. And to do so you must be where the eligible men are—"

"Aunt Louisa!" her niece broke in firmly. "If you wish to be rid of me, just say so and I'll set up my own establishment. But what I will not do is go off to London—or anywhere else, for that matter—in blatant pursuit of a husband. I know you mean well, but frankly this conversation has stiffened the resolve that my former fiancé forced upon me. I will not marry for the 'convenience' of an unfaithful spouse. Oh, I don't doubt you're right in one respect. It would be naive of me to expect a love match. And by the by, I don't really think of myself as a heroine out of one of those novels you think so little of. But since I don't have to marry for financial reasons, I see no point—" Lady Venetia broke off here, aware that her aunt was no longer attending.

Lady Stoke was leaning forward on the edge of the settee, squinting through the crowd at a new arrival. Venetia looked in the direction of her aunt's narrowed gaze. It was targeted upon a portly gentleman in a bright-blue tailcoat who was staring at the assembly through a quizzing glass.

"Why, I do believe it's Porge! Porge Carstairs!" Lady

Stoke exclaimed. "Yes, it's bound to be. Who else would wear such a monstrous buttonhole this time of year? What did I tell you, Venetia?" her ladyship crowed as she rose to her feet, waving her hand in circles above her head to draw the gentleman's attention. "Sooner or later every gentleman a bit beyond my own age bracket either comes here on his own accord or is sent here by his quack. Oh, famous! He's seen me!"

Indeed, the quizzing glass held steady, a huge smile split the corpulent face, and then the gentleman came bearing down upon them as fast as a rather mincing gait would allow.

"Would you look at that," Lady Stoke hissed in her niece's ear. "What did I tell you? Case of gout or I'm a Dutchman."

"Louisa, by gad, it is you!" The gentleman, panting a bit from so much exertion, beamed down at her ladyship. "What a stroke of luck! Had begun to think there was no company worth bothering with in Bath, and here you are, like something fetched up by a genie from a bottle. You're a sight for sore eyes, gel. Lovely as always." Lady Stoke was being smothered in a bearlike embrace while her niece looked on curiously.

What she saw was an elderly gentleman whose immense girth and thinning hair had by no means diminished his propensity for dandyism. Even brighter than his coat was its nosegay of flowers. Canary pantaloons strained across his stomach and hugged his bulging thighs. Hessian boots gleamed like mirrors, their tassels brilliant gold. Shirt points starched stiff as plaster forced his several chins upon an upward slant. He was just saved from appearing ludicrous, Venetia decided, by an expression as amiable as his apparel was affected. After an enthusiastic buss upon the cheek, the gentleman released her aunt and turned his interested gaze to Venetia as Lady Stoke made the introductions.

"M'dear, allow me to present one of my oldest and dearest friends, Sir George Carstairs. Porge, this is Lady Venetia Lowther, me brother Victor's daughter. You remember Victor, of course."

"Charmed, m'dear." Sir George bent over Venetia's hand as gallantly as the creak of his corsets would allow. "Knew your father slightly. Didn't move in the same circles, though. He was younger than me, for one thing. And too brainy by half. Always studying something or other. Couldn't've been less like Louisa here. But then families are that way. Take me own brother, for instance—"

"Oh, do let's sit down, Porge dear," Lady Stoke interrupted. "Is it gout?" She gestured toward the foot he was favoring. "I thought as much," she continued, her diagnosis having been confirmed. "And you will insist upon wearing those tight Hessians in spite of all your sufferings. Well, I cannot say I blame you, for you always were all the crack, Porge. A regular Brummell. And one should never allow minor infirmities to force a lowering of standards. But still, there's no need to stand around when we can be comfortable." She spied a group leaving a nearby table. "Oh, good. There's an empty place. Now we can all sit together and have a coze. Do hurry before some other party claims it."

"Oh, but that's not necessary," Venetia quickly interposed. "Let Sir George sit here beside you on the settee. I know you old friends have a great deal to talk of, and this will give me the opportunity to visit the circulating library without feeling guilty about deserting you, Aunt Louisa." She smiled mischievously. "I need to replenish my supply of those dreadful novels that you've been at pains to warn me against."

The old friends watched her departing back in silence. ''Demmed fine-looking gel.'' Sir George pronounced his verdict once Venetia had left the room. ''Can't hold a candle to her aunt, of course,'' he added gallantly, ''but you've no call to blush for her, m'dear. No cause at all.''

Lady Stoke fastened her large blue eyes intently upon him. ''You ain't just doing the polite, are you, Porge? You do really mean it?''

''About the gel not holding a candle to her aunt? Of course I mean it,'' he declared a shade too heartily. ''Why, you don't look a day over thirty, Louisa. No, by gad, make that twenty-nine.''

''Oh, for heaven's sake, Porge dear, I was not referring to all that fustian about me. Although you mustn't think I'm indifferent to it. I'll gladly accept all the Spanish coin you care to fling my way. But not right at this moment. Now I'm concerned merely with Venetia. Did you mean it when you said that she's attractive?''

''Of course I meant it. It's obvious enough, I'd say. Neat figure, nice expression. And that combination of fair hair and dark eyes is most striking. The girl's no diamond of the first water, perhaps, but well above average certainly.''

''Would men think so?''

''What the devil's that supposed to mean? What do you take me for, a cabbage?''

''Don't dissemble, Porge. You know exactly what I'm asking. Anybody can decide whether a female's features are all they should be and if her complexion's up to snuff. But what I want to know is, would a man look at her in that certain way? Oh, botheration! Why am I being so missish with you, of all people? What I want to know is, would you wish to go to bed with her?''

Sir George was shocked. ''Good gad, Louisa, have you

lost your mind? The idea's monstrous. Why, the gel's barely out of leading strings.''

''She's twenty-four when it comes to that, but of course I don't mean you specifically. I was speaking figuratively. I merely wish to know if you think men in general would find her appealing in that way.''

''Someone's bound to. At least in my experience, coves find all sorts of odd females attractive. Not to say that your niece is odd,'' he clarified. ''Merely making the point that if freakish females can find men who wish to bed 'em, certainly your Venetia can. But what the devil are you up to, Louisa? This kind of talk ain't quite the thing, you know.''

''I do know, Porge.'' Lady Stoke sighed heavily. ''But you see, I'm quite determined to do something about Venetia. Indeed, I *have* to do something about Venetia before she drives me to distraction.''

''My word! Like that, is it?'' Sir George's eyes widened in surprise. ''Seemed a pleasant-enough chit. But then you never know.''

''Oh, she is quite pleasant. You must not jump to the wrong conclusion, Porge. I like the girl prodigiously. Why, I couldn't think more highly of her if she was me own daughter. Though it's hard to imagine that this conversation would be necessary if she was. The thing is, George—'' And Lady Stoke proceeded to fill her friend in on the details of Venetia's broken engagement.

''I don't understand any of it,'' she concluded, shaking her head in bewilderment, setting the roses on her bonnet into motion. ''You see, it seems to me, Porge, that if Venetia was really up to snuff where the male sex is concerned and if she was bothered by the fact her fiancé was supporting a mistress, she should have had no difficulty at all in persuading him to send the trollop packing—for the first few months, at least, by which time she might be just as glad to see her reinstalled. But not only did Venetia refuse to put up a fight for the man she was betrothed to, but she's quite determined to be an old maid. And what's worse, she's going to be it here with me!

"Oh, Porge, Venetia is the kindest thing." Lady Stoke's countenance was stricken. "She cossets me. She's solicitous. She fetches things. I swear it, Porge, I've never felt so *old*. There, now. I've said it. The thing is, I've never, ever wanted a companion. But if I did desire one, it would be some female of my own age or older who would not make me feel like Methuselah. I vow, Porge, it should not surprise you if any day now you see Venetia pushing me down Stall Street in a Bath chair!"

"My God!" Her friend was horrified by the outburst. "Send the chit packing!"

"No, Porge dear, I can't do that. I will not hurt her feelings. For I really do like the girl, you see. And she's suffered a most severe blow. To her pride, if not her heart, which might take longer to heal, actually. No, Porge, what I wish to do is marry Venetia off. That's why I asked your opinion of her desirability. For it would be best if I could find someone to fall in love with her. Frankly, I don't think she'll tolerate being courted a second time just for her fortune."

"Well, if the fellow's worth his salt, she wouldn't have to know it."

"That's so, of course. But the immediate problem is to find some eligible males to throw at her head. She refuses to go to London and, well, just look around you." Lady Stoke repeated the sweeping gesture with which she'd earlier dismissed Bath's male population. "You're the only attractive male in the whole assemblage, Porge, and I quite refuse to share you with Venetia."

Sir George *pshaw*ed the compliment but looked pleased by it all the same as he bent his none-too-powerful intellect upon the problem. "Why, it's simply another case of the mountain and Mohomet, m'dear," he pronounced after a few moments' thought. "That's it, pure and simple."

"I beg your pardon?"

"You must know the saying."

Since apparently Lady Stoke did not, he went on to enlighten her. "If the mountain won't come to Mohomet, Mohomet must go to the mountain, or some such thing."

"Don't you have that backward? But never mind, for really, Porge, I don't see what bearing some heathen proverb has on Venetia's problem. The girl will be back here any moment. I don't need senseless sayings. I need advice."

"I'm giving it," he explained patiently. "Simply trying to say that if there ain't any young men to be had in Bath, you'll have to import 'em."

"And just how am I expected to do that, pray tell? You don't order up a dozen eligible young bachelors like oysters."

"Don't need a dozen, actually. One will do for starters."

"Well, I don't have one. That is to say, not one I know well enough to ask down here on his own. Too obvious, anyhow. Venetia wouldn't sit still for it. I suppose I could give a house party." Her face assumed a martyred look. "Though I'd hate it above all things. No, we'd best dismiss that notion. It won't do. No one under fifty would come to a house party held in Bath."

"No need to have a party. Send for Wincanton. The very ticket."

"Wincanton?"

"Oh, come now, Louisa. Surely you ain't forgotten your heir."

"Of course not. I've also not forgotten that he's been in the army for donkey's years. With Wellington. Chasing Bonaparte. In Belgium or some such place, the last I heard."

"Well, he ain't there now. Friend of mine saw him in Brooks' just last week. Said he's quit the army. Nothing left to do now. Surely, Louisa, you must've heard of Waterloo. Even in Bath."

"Gareth Wincanton's in London? Oh, Porge, it just might do at that. But do you think he'd come?"

"I think he'll have to if you ask him," the other replied simply. "Got no choice. Duty-bound, you know."

"Me, ask him? Oh, no, I think not." The world was looking a great deal rosier to Lady Stoke. "I'll do better than that!" She clapped her hands and crowed. "For it pays to be subtle in these things, Porge dear. I'll simply let his mother do it."

Chapter Two

*T*he party gathered around the punch bowl in a private
parlor at Brooks' Club in London could not be described as "convivial," in spite of the fact that the four
gentlemen had been drinking deep. The problem was that
both the host and his special guest were decidedly blue-
deviled. This twosome, along with their companions, had
come to the exclusive club directly from Drury Lane Theatre for the specific purpose of shooting the cat. But the
punch, though potent, had not had the desired effect of
lifting the party's spirits.

The host, Major Gareth Wincanton, late of His Majesty's cavalry, had perhaps the greater claim to an acute case
of the dismals. Affairs of the heart are traditionally given

precedence over other kinds of woes, such as suddenly losing one's source of livelihood, as was the case with Mr. Nicholas Forbes, his guest.

In the ordinary way of things, Major Wincanton and Mr. Forbes would not have been thrown together socially. And certainly in the ordinary way of things Mr. Forbes would not have been admitted into a gentlemen's club, since by no stretch of the imagination did he qualify for that high honor. Indeed, the only degree of merriment the party had thus far managed to achieve came from recalling how Mr. Forbes had been foisted off as Major Wincanton's cousin. "Distant" cousin, actually, was the nearest relationship that the major had been able to force himself to claim. Then, perhaps to make up for such halfheartedness, he'd gone on to add that he and his "cousin" had had the honor to serve in the same regiment. This embellishment was almost their undoing, for it sent his cronies off into sudden spasms, since they all knew that while the statement was literally true, the major had served on Wellington's staff, whereas Mr. Forbes had been the merest ranker.

It was a capricious fate that had thrown these two unlikely candidates for comradeship together. Fate in the guise of the comely, provocative romantic leading lady of Drury Lane, Miss Amabel Fawnhope, who was lusted after by Major Wincanton and "sister" to Mr. Forbes.

For shortly after selling his commission and arriving back in London, Major Wincanton had attended a performance of *The Fatal Marriage*, gazed down upon a black-haired, violet-eyed goddess, and lost his head completely. And it had come as a severe blow to his self-esteem when his suit had failed to prosper. The major had never before been rebuffed by any female of a certain stamp, which was the only type of female he pursued, having no desire to forfeit a bachelorhood he was enjoying to the hilt. Wincanton was personable, he was rich, he was an earl's grandson and a war hero—a combination that should have assured him spontaneous success. But in the case of Miss Fawnhope, actress, it had failed to do so.

Not that Miss Fawnhope spurned him. Far from it. She was warm and caring and in their more tender moments had been known to whisper words of deep affection into his ear. The rub was, Miss Amabel Fawnhope drew the line at consummating their relationship, and none of the major's considerable powers of seduction had thus far been able to break down her iron-willed resistance. She had even breached the rules of conduct generally accepted in this type of situation by hinting broadly that marriage would be the only means to the major's desired ends. A circumstance that was, of course, quite unthinkable.

It was after his courtship had reached this impasse that Major Wincanton had begun to cultivate Mr. Forbes, who was as close to being family as Miss Fawnhope could claim. It was the major's hope that Forbes, a rather rackety here-and-thereian but a man of the world nonetheless, could make Amabel see reason. Now even this support was about to be taken from him.

"What are you going to do now, Nicky?" he asked. Recalled to his hostly duties, he refilled the others' punch cups.

"Damned if I know." Forbes shrugged. "Head for the provinces, I expect. Put in a season or so there. Then maybe Covent Garden can use me."

"Rotten luck, old man," said "Sprig" St. Leger, corpulent and thirty, who was so named not for his youth or size but for his fashion excesses. "Terrible thing, getting booted out like that. Unfair. Didn't think you were all that bad myself.''

"Don't read the notices, then, do you?''

This comment—from the fourth member of the company, Owen, Lord Piggot-Jones, an effete-looking young man with pale eyes, pale skin, pale hair—earned Piggot-Jones a darkling look from the actor, who was sensitive about his reviews. "Mr. Forbes's lack of histrionic talent was mercilessly exposed by the beacon of Kean's brilliance,'' the *Times*'s critic had observed.

"Nicky's performance had nothing to say in the matter,'' Wincanton interposed diplomatically. "His looks were his problem. You know how sensitive Kean is about his height—his appearance in general, for that matter. He's not about to let someone tall and handsome share the stage with him.''

Nicky Forbes gave his host a grateful look, but the Sprig, who was more than a bit disguised, had a fit of the giggles that ended up in hiccoughs. "You only say so, Wincanton,'' he finally managed, "because you two are dead ringers for each other. Just a roundabout way of puffing your own self up, if you ask me.''

This physical resemblance between the major and the private had been the subject of much discussion among the party earlier. Indeed, it had been the impetus for insinuating Nicholas Forbes into Brooks' Club in the guise of a Wincanton relative.

It was a resemblance that both involved parties publicly accepted but privately denied—the actor because he considered himself better-looking than the aristocrat, and the major because he found it intolerable to be look-alike to a Cit. "We're hardly 'dead ringers,' '' he said shortly now. "All ginger-pated coves get lumped together.''

"All ginger-pated coves don't have the same blue eyes

and cleft chins, though. By gad, it's uncanny.'' The Sprig became convulsed once more as an idea struck him. ''You sure you two ain't actually cousins after all? Or brothers, even? Oh, I say, Win, could it be that you ain't the first of your family to lose your head over some actress? How about it, Nicky? Tell us—who's your father?''

The Sprig's face turned a deep, dark red as the actor leveled him with a set-down look that the great Kean himself might have envied. ''Sorry,'' Mr. St. Leger mumbled. ''Devilish poor taste.''

Nicky nodded a curt acceptance of the apology while mentally examining, then rejecting, the other's insinuation. He could come up with three—or possibly four—good candidates for the post of his progenitor. Not one of these had the slightest Wincanton connection.

''You couldn't stick around London for a fortnight or so longer, could you, Nicky?'' The actor's dubious parentage held no fascination for the major. His mind had reverted to his own problems. ''Perhaps Amabel could—'' He cut himself short, then shied away from the suggestion he was about to make, that Miss Fawnhope would most likely be happy to house Nicky temporarily. Somehow the idea of those two living together held little appeal to him, even though they'd done so as children. ''Amabel will miss you,'' he amended.

''I doubt that. She won't have time.''

''Oh, God, you're right. And I'd counted on you to act as a sort of chaperon to keep the other coves away while I'm gone. Of all the curst luck.'' Wincanton gave a heartfelt groan, then ladled out more punch to one and all. ''As if it weren't bad enough to have to leave London myself just when Amabel was beginning to come around, now you won't be here either to protect my interests. That swine Leacock's just waiting for me to turn my back so he can make his move. Of all the damnable timing, this has to be the worst.''

"Oh, you're going away, Win?" Lord Piggot-Jones stopped drinking deep to ask.

"My God, Owen, where have you been all evening?" the Sprig inquired. "Win's off to Bath. That's what this wake's all about, for heaven's sake."

"Bath? Why on earth would anybody go to Bath? Last place I'd want to go, I'll tell you."

"I don't *want* to go," Wincanton said impatiently. "I *have* to go. My father insists I pay a duty visit to Lady Stoke. I'm the heir, you see."

The others, with the exception of Mr. Forbes, murmured sympathetically.

"Cut you off without a shilling, would she, if you didn't show?" the actor asked.

"Oh, no. She can't do that, actually. It's her husband's fortune. Or was. He's dead, of course. No, it isn't that. It's just that the old lady's heard I'm out of the army and her nose is out of joint that I've not been to see her. Don't know why it should be. She hasn't clapped eyes on me since I was at Eton. But if she wants me, I'll have to go. Devilish bad ton not to, you know. Besides," he added, "if I don't go do the polite, my father will be coming to London to learn the reason why. And that's all that's needed. I can imagine the dust-up when he discovers I'm dangling after an actress. Waterloo won't touch it for fireworks. Oh, lord, what a coil."

"Well, look on the bright side." Piggot-Jones spoke soothingly. "Since Nicky here's being banished, too, you two could travel down together. Or does Bath have a theater, Nicky? Wouldn't surprise me any if it didn't."

"Well, yes, as a matter of fact. Quite a good one, actually. The Theatre Royal. Come to think on it, that would be as good a place to start as any—especially if I can wheedle a ride, Major." He brightened at the thought of the savings in coach fare.

"I've a better idea!" The Sprig, who was most definitely castaway, clapped his hands with sudden inspiration. "Why don't you go in his place?"

"I beg your pardon?"

"Of course! Why didn't we think of it before? It's the very thing. You have to leave London. Win don't want to. You take his place."

"You really must be foxed, St. Leger." Despite this observation, Wincanton poured them all more punch.

"No, I ain't. At least foxed's got nothing to say in the matter. You coves are the ones who must be disguised past all reasoning. Use your noggins, why don't you? What have we just been talking about? That you two are dead ringers for each other, that's what. Oh, very well, then," he reacted to his host's expression, "maybe you ain't just alike precisely, but there is a decided resemblance, you can't deny. And didn't you just say that your aunt, Lady Whosoever, hasn't seen you since your school days? Well, then, there you are."

"Where exactly are we?" Wincanton asked sarcastically.

"I'm simply trying to point out that there'd be nothing to it. What's the old lady going to remember about you? The color of your hair, that's what. And maybe after that, your eyes. And they're near enough a match with Nicky's. My dear fellow, no one, but no one, looks the same as he did during his school days. And thank God for it." He shuddered. "Nothing but a mass of spots back then myself."

Wincanton was beginning to look thoughtful. "Well, I'll grant you," he said grudgingly, "that he might get by with an impersonation as far as appearance alone goes. But he couldn't pull off the rest in a million years.''

''Why not? Knows you too well, does she? Your aunt, I mean.''

''No, that's not it. Aunt Louisa and I were never together all that much. She was Uncle's second wife. After he died, she married again. So Aunt Louisa was never all that close to our family, actually.''

''Well, then, there you are,'' the Sprig pronounced thickly. ''She ain't likely to be dragging up odd bits of your family history, then, that Nicky here wouldn't know about. And if she asked about some of your kith and kin, he could simply make up the answers and she'd not know the difference. And if he did get stumped on something or other''—his enthusiasm mounted—''he could fall back on the war. He could claim that the whole horrible business of Waterloo wiped everything else out of his memory. Happens, you know. By Jove!'' He tried to snap his fingers, but they just missed making contact. ''It all fits. You were wounded, weren't you, Win?''

''Yes, as a matter of fact. In the leg. Which hardly makes me a candidate for loss of memory.''

''Where you were hit ain't the point, old man,'' Mr. St. Leger explained patiently. ''It's the horror of battle you wished to wipe out of your mind. And in managing that, you just overdid a bit, that's all, and wiped out a lot of other stuff as well.''

''Don't be an ass, Sprig.'' The major, a consummate soldier, had never had the slightest desire to wipe out one moment of a military engagement that had changed the course of history.

''Oh, well, then, if that's the way you feel about it.'' The Sprig sulked a moment, but was loath to abandon the

22

idea. "Well, then, look at the thing another way," he tried again. "What's the thing that you and Nicky here have in common? Besides Miss Fawnhope, that is. The war. Waterloo. My word, you both go all the way back to the Battle of Salamanca, don't you? Well, then, that's it. What else does anyone want to hear about? Females especially. Anytime the conversation gets a bit sticky, he can talk about the war. Safe as houses." He looked around the table in a challenging manner. Lord Piggot-Jones hiccoughed and nodded.

"Well, then, there you are." The Sprig was enjoying his role as barrister. "You don't want to go to Bath. Nicky's an out-of-work actor needing a part. Hire him to play you, and all's right and tight for both you chaps."

Nicholas's befogged mind had tended to wander somewhat during the exchange, but the word "hire" now gained his full attention.

Wincanton was thinking. Then after a pregnant pause he shook his head. "No, I tell you. It would never work."

"And why wouldn't it?" the Sprig asked.

Major Wincanton looked embarrassed. "Beg pardon, Nicky. Don't wish to appear offensive, but what I mean to say is, there's the *gentleman* thing, you know. It's not just something a cove can assume. He has to *be*."

"For heaven's sake, Win, the man's an actor!"

The word seemed to hang suspended in the air while each member of the party examined it, two recalling the performance they'd just witnessed, another remembering the reviews. Mr. Forbes, who despite his state of advanced intoxication missed nothing of the general reaction, looked miffed.

"St. Leger's right, dammit. I am an actor! Oh, I know what you're all thinking. That I ain't been exactly the critics' darling. But on the other hand"—he gave the major a haughty look that was intensified by the fact he was seeing two of him—"if you don't mind me saying so, Major Wincanton, you ain't exactly Hamlet the Dane, you know. What I mean to say is, I could play you in a breeze. Nothing to it. All a cove would have to do is stare right through common folk and never see 'em and talk like a toff, then limp a bit to peg down your character. Why, I'd be willing to wager anybody that aunt of yours would be calling me 'nephew' in no time flat.''

"So would I!'' the Sprig chimed in. "Look at it this way. We passed him off as a gentleman here, didn't we? And I'm sure your aunt can't be any more of a high stickler than our Charles is. By Jove, I'm sure Nicky can do it. And I've got a thousand pounds that says Nicholas can impersonate you, Win.''

At the magic word "wager," Piggot-Jones had come to life. What had merely been an academic discussion, and a fairly boring one at that, now took on all the heady elements of a horse race or a boxing mill. "Oh, I say, if Forbes here did take your place, Win, how long would he have to do it?''

Nicholas thought the question amazingly intelligent, considering the source.

"Why, for the whole of February. You see, I'm supposed to squire Aunt Louisa around to the assembly rooms, take her to the theater, that sort of thing.''

The actor, who had been thinking more in terms of a fortnight, stifled a groan. But his professional pride, which had taken a severe drubbing of late, reasserted itself. "Since this is just another acting job far as I'm concerned, what would it pay?''

"What do actors earn?'' Wincanton countered.

Mr. Forbes gave the matter thought, then, without

blushing, came up with a figure that would have caused a star of Drury Lane to jump for joy.

"Well, then, how about it, Win? Is it worth that much blunt to you to stay here in London and storm Miss Fawnhope's citadel and repel all other boarders?" the Sprig inquired in a clash of metaphors.

A long draft of the powerful punch made up the major's mind for him. "Yes, by gad, it is!"

"Well, then, I'll take your wager, Sprig," Lord Piggot-Jones declared. "My thousand pounds against yours that Forbes here will be unmasked long before a month's up."

To Nicky's disgust, St. Leger hesitated as if his brain had suddenly unclouded. His "Done!" when he finally uttered it and extended his hand lacked the true ring of conviction to his listeners' ears.

"You don't sound too confident, Sprig," Wincanton observed dryly.

The actor was stung by his champion's sudden attack of cravenness. A man had his pride, by Jove. "He has no cause for concern, Major. By George, I'm more than eager to back my own performance. What would you say to a thousand pounds?"

This reckless bravado was aimed at Wincanton, who merely arched an eyebrow at the notion of the actor commanding that kind of blunt.

It was Lord Piggot-Jones who shouted "Done, by God!" and stuck out a hand. And before Nicky could retract his question, his own fist was being pumped vigorously up and down.

The Sprig motioned to a waiter who'd been hovering nearby, hoping the party would soon go home. The betting book was fetched and the wagers duly entered.

Mr. Nicholas Forbes was of a sudden sober and feeling more than a trifle ill. It was all that he could manage not to cast up his accounts right then and there in Brooks' exclusive club for gentlemen.

Chapter
Three

The pounding on her door finally penetrated the dream of Miss Amabel Fawnhope. She was standing before an altar, plighting her troth. Though the face of her bridegroom kept perversely changing, there was no doubt at all of the most salient fact: He possessed both rank and fortune.

Miss Fawnhope murmured a futile "I do," then reluctantly cracked open her lids and squinted at the day. It was morning, sure enough, but what o'clock? She opened her eyes wider and focused on the ormolu timepiece that had the place of honor on her bedchamber mantel. Eight! Who would dare? The pounding increased. "Gareth!" she breathed, her eyes taking on some of the sparkle that made them so appealing by stage candlelight. She reached for the dressing gown draped around the bedpost and hurried eagerly toward the sound.

Her face fell as she unlocked the door. "Oh, it's you."

"Well, thanks ever so much." Nicholas Forbes entered her small hallway. "And it's nice to see you, too, love."

"Oh, don't be so goosish, Nicky." Miss Fawnhope rose on tiptoe to plant a kiss upon his cheek that did very little to mollify him. "It's just that I—"

"I know. You were expecting someone else." He made no effort to sound less aggrieved.

"Well, you are the last person in the world I'd expect to rouse a working actress from her beauty sleep. Oh, heavens, Nicky, I didn't mean . . . Don't look like that. I wasn't thinking."

" 'Working actress.' That's right, Bella. Go on. Throw it in my teeth." Martyrdom sat heavily upon him. "You're the only employed member of this family now. I'm well aware of that."

"Oh, for pity's sake, Nicky, don't be so touchy. Here I haven't seen you for three whole days, and I've been worried about you. Come sit down. I'll ring for tea. I just hope the shock won't kill Nellie. She ain't used to any exertion before noon."

It said a lot for Miss Fawnhope's rapid rise in the theatrical world that at the age of twenty she could hire a house in Russell Street and keep a maid. True, the rent on the former was often in arrears, and the latter, an out-of-work actress in her declining years, was more than content to take on her less-than-rigorous duties merely for her keep. Still, Nicky thought with a stab of jealousy as he looked around the little parlor, which was charmingly, if cheaply, furnished with secondhand pieces and some stage

28

discards, there was no denying the fact that Amabel was doing well. Very well indeed.

As the maid came in, bearing a tray that gave off a promising aroma and a cloud of steam, Nicky continued to gaze around himself, partly to avoid looking at Nellie, who was putting the tray down with a thump while muttering darkly about folk who ought to know better than to rob an actress of her much-needed sleep, not even to mention servants what stayed up to all hours to do their duty by the young, who had no proper notion of what it was like to be old and feeble, thinking old age was a condition as would never happen to the likes of them.

"Oh, do go on back to bed," Amabel said with a sigh, "and quit jawing at poor Nicky here. He's got trouble enough without you ringing a peal over him, too."

"Don't I know it." Nellie, who had known both the young people since their leading-string days, suddenly forgot her own grievances and looked fondly at the young man. "But never you mind, Nicky darling. Any man as 'eartbreaking 'andsome as you've turned out is bound to get back up on the stage. Talent be blowed. It's looks what counts. As others in this room can testify.

"Of course, now," she pontificated as she poured out the steaming brew into mismatched cups, "that scoundrel Kean is the exception what proves the rule. All he's got is talent. Jealous as anything of you, Nicky, the mean-spirited scapegallows." She yawned prodigiously. "Well, I'm off to bed again. Never you fret, Nicky love. Something will turn up for you. It's bound to." The words were more optimistic than the doleful shake she gave the gray head under the dirty nightcap as she left the room.

"How do you put up with the old harridan?" Nicky kept his voice low as he picked up his cup and took a restoring swallow.

"How can you ask? She was your mother's closest friend, in case you've forgotten. Besides"—Amabel dimpled fetchingly—"she's useful when I need a chaperon."

"Which is most of the time, I don't doubt." Nicky sized up his "sister" from across the tea table with the eye of a connoisseur. It still amazed him that the scrawny brat he'd known when he'd enlisted in the army ten years before had turned into this beauty. Even though he'd managed to see her from time to time on his infrequent leaves (including a fortnight when his mother had died and he'd arranged for Nellie to keep an eye on the child), he'd not been prepared for this transformation. Bella was a nonpareil, no mistake.

She grew aware of his intense appraisal and pulled her dressing gown, which carelessly exposed an improper amount of creamy bosom, more decorously around her. "For heaven's sake, Nicky, put your eyes back in your head," she said reproachfully. "Surely I don't have to stand on points with you."

"You don't have to watch your manners, if that's what you mean," he answered shortly. "But you'd do well to keep your clothes on. I'm male and human, for God's sake."

"But you're family!"

"If you say so."

"I do say so!" The gorgeous violet eyes were intensely serious. "You're my big brother, Nicky. That's the most important thing in the world to me, so don't you ever forget it. And I was sure you felt the same. Why, you've always been there for me—even when you weren't," she continued with a total lack of logic. "I mean I always knew I had a *family*, as long as there was you. Can you understand that, Nicky?"

Well, yes, he supposed he could if he was forced to.

Amabel's father had been just one more in a steady succession of lovers whom his actress mother had enjoyed during her foreshortened lifetime. The only thing that separated him from the other "uncles," in Nicky's mind, was that when he had moved in with them he had brought along a tiny daughter and when he had moved out he had left her behind, neither of which occurrences perturbed Nicky's mother in the least. Little Amabel was simply absorbed into their third-rate touring company, with Nicky given responsibility for the child when his mother was otherwise engaged, which was most of the time. He bearled her and she adored him, an arrangement that suited him quite well.

But after his discharge from the army, he had a great deal of difficulty in dealing with their changed status. Even the fact that Amabel had wheedled the manager of Drury Lane into hiring him had been something of a pill to swallow, although at the same time he was grateful.

Her success with the opposite sex had been even harder to contend with than her theatrical achievements, perhaps because his self-acknowledged jealousy had taken him completely by surprise. Now, as he dipped one of the light wigs Nellie had supplied into the steamy tea, he looked around him with a jaundiced eye. Every table in the room was abloom with flowers. "This place looks like a curst hothouse. Can't imagine how you ever manage to breathe. You would think that some of your nabobs could put their blunt to better use. Why don't they give you something that don't die off right away? Something you could hock."

"It's not *they*. It's *he*. Major Wincanton. And he sends flowers because I've told him they're the only gifts that I'll accept," Amabel said.

"Are you daft? Why, the man's rich as Croesus. He could buy you anything—diamonds, pearls—you name it.

He's good for any of that stuff. Why, the major's a walking actress's old-age pension. God knows what he's worth, with more to come. Use your head, Bella.''

"Please don't call me Bella. I've told you before, it's common. And I am using my head, brother dear, because all those jewels you speak of, and carriages, too— By the by, did you know he's offered to buy me a curricle with a pair of matched grays to pull it?''

Nicky's eyes opened wide, followed by his mouth. He knew exactly the kind of rig she referred to. He'd left a similar one around the corner with a small disgruntled tiger in charge of it.

"But you see, Nicky,'' Amabel continued, "all those gifts have strings attached, and I'm not interested.'' She directed a small, complacent smile toward her teacup. "You see, I mean to marry Major Wincanton.''

"Don't be a fool.''

Nicky had spoken much too sharply and instantly regretted it as the actress raised her chin and gave him a frigid look.

"I'm sorry, Bella—Amabel—for such plain speaking. But you'd best get it into your head that the Wincantons of this world don't marry the likes of you. Oh, I know he's besotted.'' He waved his hand to take in the bouquets of flowers. "But not beyond all reason. He's a swell, Bella. A toff. Stiff-rumped as they make 'em. And he ain't likely to forget his obligations to his family. Or to his class, when it comes to that. No, the major won't marry someone off the stage.''

"It's been known to happen.''

"Yes, on rare occasions. And usually by young sprigs of the nobility too green to know what's what. I tell you for your own good, Bella. I know Wincanton, and he's too fly by half to let himself be leg-shackled to a Cit, no matter how in love he fancies himself.''

''Oh?'' She tossed her tousled dark curls and her brilliant eyes flashed, and for just a moment his deep conviction began to waver. To him she had never appeared lovelier than in this early-morning dishabille, with her hair tumbling every which way and her well-worn dressing gown inclined to slip its moorings. As far as he was concerned, all the regal gowns and paste jewelry she'd worn on stage couldn't touch her present costume for desirability. If Gareth Wincanton had seen her like this, God knew what the upshot would be. No! He pulled himself up short. No use both of them becoming bird-witted. He was right. Wincanton would never marry Amabel, and that was that.

Disconcertingly, she read his mind. ''Would you care to make a wager?''

''I would not!'' After the fiasco at Brooks' Club, Nicky had sworn off betting. He came close to breaking out in a cold sweat once again as the image of his signature in that betting book came floating before his eyes.

With an effort he changed tack and adopted a more conciliatory tone. ''Look, I don't enjoy being the one to have to say you've got maggots in your head. But I don't want to see you hurt, love. And you will be if you go on thinking the major will marry you.''

''He'll marry me if it's the only way he can get what he wants. And believe me, it is.''

Amabel Fawnhope was a stage phenomenon—a desirable young woman whose looks were her greatest asset but who still managed to keep her manager, her fellow actors, and an adoring public at arm's length. Shortly after arriving back in London from the Continent, Nicholas himself had made a halfhearted attempt at seduction, feeling slightly incestuous at the time, and had had an ear-boxing followed by a good tongue-lashing.

"I think your scheme would work," he now conceded, "on almost any other of those gentry coves who are dangling after you. But not Wincanton. You'll never bring him up to scratch. Why not switch to someone else?"

"You don't like him much, do you?"

This was a question he'd not previously bothered to think about, but no, by Jupiter, he guessed he didn't. "What I think of the major's got nothing to say in the matter," he replied aloud. "The thing is, Bella, I know the man, and he's as high in the instep as they come. But you could do worse," he went on seriously, partly from a reluctant conviction and partly because he'd agreed to do so before he'd parted from Wincanton, "than to let him set you up in style somewhere. The man's not exactly my cup of tea, I grant you, but he ain't tightfisted. He'd see you fixed for life. I'd stake my own on that."

"He'll see me fixed for life, all right." Miss Fawnhope leaned toward him. "But not the way you mean. I intend to marry, Nicky. I'm *determined* to. You, of all people, should appreciate that ambition. We've both seen enough of the other kind of life. And I'm not having it."

"You surely ain't comparing being set up by Wincanton with the life my mother led."

"A mistress is still a mistress, while a wife's a wife," she said stubbornly. "But enough of this. Let's change the subject. It's not my affairs that need discussing; it's yours. What do you plan to do, Nicky? You can move in here, of course."

"No, that's what I can't do, Bella."

And even if there had been no wager, he still could not have done so. For though he was not averse to being a sponge under other circumstances, the notion of letting

34

Amabel support him was somehow unthinkable—a leftover, no doubt, from the period in their lives when she hero-worshipped him. "Thanks anyhow, Bella, but I'm off for Bath. Just stopped to say good-bye, as a matter of fact."

"The Theatre Royal? That's a famous idea! Mr. Powell's down there, did you know? He was Mama's special friend when we played Bristol years ago, remember? He's bound to put in a good word for you."

It took all Nicky's self-control not to wince at that piece of news. Well, he'd just have to put a wide berth between himself and the theater, that's all.

"Would it help if I wrote the manager there?" Amabel asked.

"It might, but I'd rather you didn't," he replied rather shortly.

"Hoity-toity! You are the proud one, aren't you? And you call Major Wincanton high in the instep! Well"—she looked him over carefully—"I doubt my say-so would make much difference anyhow. And even if I was another Mrs. Siddons, it'd still be unnecessary. Just look at you. You've 'leading man' written all over you. And where did you find your new tailor? I've never seen you looking so bang-up-to-the-nines." She gazed with approval at the bottle-green coat he wore along with fawn-colored breeches and white-topped black boots. "If I didn't know better, I'd say Weston made that coat." In truth the famous Bond Street tailor *had* done so—for Major Gareth Wincanton, however.

"You should have no trouble getting hired, Nicky. Of course, you may have to work backstage awhile till the proper part comes along.

"Do you know," she continued thoughtfully, "this could all be for the best in the long run? You getting the sack here, I mean. A season or so in the provinces won't do you any harm. It'll give you a chance to really learn your craft.''

''What do you mean, 'learn my craft'?'' he said, bristling. ''I was shoved onstage soon as I could toddle, the same as you.''

''Lor' love us, ain't we touchy!'' She threw up her arms in mock dismay. ''The difference between us, brother dear, was that I wanted to perform and you fought it all the way. Why, you could hardly wait to run off to the army. Whatever possessed you, Nicky, to give the theater another try?''

''I learned an important lesson while fighting for my country.'' He grinned a crooked smile. ''The worst they throw at actors is rotten oranges, which beats cannonballs and bullets by a mile.''

She laughed. ''Oh, but you were so heroic-looking in your uniform. And you *were* heroic, I've been told.''

Nicky tried to look modest, which actually wasn't all that difficult, since he entertained a certain ambivalence about his military exploits. He certainly had no cause to blush for his service record. He'd been as brave as any man whose chief objective was to emerge from the conflict alive could be, he supposed. But heroic? Never!

''Anyhow,'' Amabel was saying, ''I can see why it suited you to leave the army now the fighting's over. But you could have knocked me down with a feather when you decided to come back on the stage. There are other choices, you know.''

''Such as?'' He rose to his feet. ''Name one, Bella, that doesn't involve grubbing for a living and I'll consider it. But in the meantime, I'm off.''

''Oh, Nicky!'' Amabel wailed. ''I will miss you.'' She jumped up and ran around the table in order to plaster herself against him in a manner he found most disconcerting. "I'd just got used to having you around again"—she sniffled into his shoulder—"and now you're leaving. It's just like it was before, when I thought I'd die of it." Her eyes were full of tears as she raised her face to look reproachfully at him. Nicky bent down and kissed her.

Vaguely he had intended for the kiss to be brotherly. But the whole thing got out of hand. His lips were soon traveling with a feverish intensity from her lips to her ear, by way of her cheek, then down her throat; they had targeted her breast when he was given a fierce push and sent careening back against the door.

"Nicky!"

He was glad to note that she, too, was breathing heavily, and not just from the exertion of her shove.

"It's possibly a good thing you're leaving." She gathered her dressing gown around her firmly, one hand clasping the pale pink satin together underneath her chin.

"No, it wouldn't do to mess up your ambitious marriage schemes, now, would it?" He'd meant to strike a light note and had wound up sounding churlish. Lord, the critics were right. He was a lousy actor.

"No, it wouldn't." She tilted her chin defiantly. "I intend to make our fortunes, Nicky."

"*Our* fortunes?"

"Of course. We always look out for each other, don't we?"

Did they? He wasn't sure. He'd left her in the lurch before. Still, he'd always sent her a good portion of his meager pay. But urging her to let Wincanton give her a carte blanche? Damned if he knew whether that was looking out for her or not. Well, one thing was certain. It was a damned sight better for her than what he'd had foremost in his mind a moment earlier.

Nicky's hand was on the doorknob, but he turned back once more to face her. "You've not said, Bella. Tell me. Do you love him?"

"Love Gareth?" She frowned as she studied the question. "I honestly don't know. I'm not even sure what love is. Sometimes I think it's just something we've made up on the stage. I'm not sure what I feel. Oh, I won't lie to you. What I think about the most is what he can do for me—the posh life I'd lead and all of that. There are times, though, when that doesn't even enter into it and when I begin to wonder if I don't actually *love* him after all— whatever that word means. And do you know when those times are, Nicky?"

He shook his head.

"The times when he reminds me most of you."

Nicholas Forbes thought that was the most lowering statement he had ever heard.

Chapter Four

"Well, at least you ain't cow-handed."

These were the first words spoken after several miles of silence, and the first sign, albeit grudging, of approval that the diminutive tiger had accorded his bogus master.

"Why shouldn't I know horses?" Nicholas retorted. "I was in the cavalry, for God's sake."

The two were seated side by side on the leather seat of a sporting black curricle with bright yellow upholstery and wheel spokes of the same vivid color. They were traveling down the Bath Road at a rapid clip on an overcast, bone-chilling day.

"I realize you and horses are well acquainted, gov'nor,

but shoveling what comes out of one end of 'em don't necessarily qualify you to manage the bit in the teeth of the other.'' Jocko Hodges doubled up at this witticism.

Nicholas waited for him to subside. Then when the small man, who looked like a child but was actually Nicky's age, twenty-eight, finally straightened up and wiped his eyes, Nicky remarked conversationally, ''You know, sport, this scam wasn't my notion. Major Wincanton's got a bigger stake in my pulling it off than I have.'' Or he would have if I hadn't been so sap-skulled as to wager my life away, he mentally amended. ''So what I fail to understand is why the devil he had to saddle me with you.''

''That's easy enough, I'd say. To make sure you don't take this pair''—Jocko nodded toward the perfectly matched team of grays—''and head for the border with 'em. All right, all right. Just funning. No need to look so brass-faced, guv. To answer your question—somebody's got to see to the cattle, ain't they? And no telling what sort of stable old Lady Stoke may keep, or even if she keeps one. Besides, having me along gives you the proper touch of class.''

''Having you along is like carrying my own personal Jonah.''

''Watch it, guv!'' The tiger was deeply offended. ''I'll admit the major's friends greased me fist to keep 'em posted on your progress—or lack of it, most likely. But you're dicked in the nob if you think I'll blow the gab to her ladyship. Wouldn't be sporting, now, would it? Besides being completely unnecessary.'' He broke into a gap-toothed grin. ''I've ten pounds wot's said you'll land arsy-varsy without any help from me, guv.''

''Thank you for that much-needed vote of confidence.''

''I'm only telling you the God's own truth. Oh, you look

40

like the genuine article, I'll grant you.'' Jocko appraised the tall man beside him, drinking in the elegance of the major's five-caped greatcoat. "And you even talk like a gentleman. But the plain truth is"—the tiger, who was well acquainted with the other's origins, paused dramatically—"you and me has got a damned sight more in common than you and those swells you're going to be visiting has. And if they don't find you out in the first half hour, well, then I'm a Frenchy.''

Nicholas, still dwelling on the Jonah parallel, struggled with the impulse that bade him to pick up the little man and cast him overboard. He restrained himself and retreated once again into his thoughts.

They were not pleasant. Jocko Hodges had voiced only a fraction of the qualms he himself was feeling. Nor had Major Wincanton's attitude fired his confidence.

The morning after the disastrous betting at Brooks' Club, the major had sent Jocko to fetch him to St. James's Square. Nicky had been ushered into a luxurious parlor, where he'd found the major berating himself for being ten kinds of a fool. "I should never have agreed to this ramshackle scheme,'' the tirade had climaxed.

"Well, then why not call the whole thing off?" Nicky, who had had time for more than second thoughts, had considered the question reasonable but found himself impaled by a look that lost not one whit in scorn from the fact the major's eyes were bloodshot.

"That's exactly what I mean,'' Wincanton had said frostily. "A gentleman would have known better than to ask that question. We've wagered on it. The matter's closed.

"Oh, God, how could I have let myself get into such a coil?'' Wincanton had continued his self-flagellation. "Even if you should somehow manage to fool Aunt Louisa into thinking you are I—for an entire month''—he had groaned at the sheer impossibility—''just what the devil am I supposed to do when I actually do see her? Lord, I must have been totally disguised to have let myself be bamboozled into this.''

''Well''—Nicky had abandoned his own problems to give the other's serious thought—''once I've paid your duty visit, so to speak, there's no reason you should be seeing her, is there? Not for years, at any rate. And she's an old woman, didn't you say? Well, then, with luck she could pop off before the occasion ever arises.''

From Wincanton's second scornful look Nicky had concluded he'd done the ungentlemanly again. He'd found himself growing a trifle nettled. Devil take the man! Dammit, he wasn't Private Forbes anymore. He'd pulled himself up to his full height, which gave him a half-inch advantage over the aristocrat, and matched Wincanton's toplofty tone. ''Well, I doubt there are any proper rules of conduct spelled out in the gentlemen's code as to what to do if we're discovered. My own suggestion would be for you simply to deny you've ever heard of me and tough it out. But since that only makes sense, I'm sure there's an unwritten law somewhere against it. So it appears to me that we'd be well-advised to stop all this breast-beating and get on with seeing to it that I'm not found out.''

''You're right, of course,'' the major had handsomely admitted. He'd gone on to pull the bell rope and order up strong coffee. Upon its arrival he'd set to work, acquainting his pupil with details of his former life and background.

And in this area Nicky felt extremely confident. Whatever else might be lacking in his acting qualifications, he was certainly a quick study. Even as a child he'd caused his elders to marvel at how soon he was able to get his lines. So he was confident of remembering what he'd been told. It was the omissions that worried him now.

Five miles out of Bath they rested their cattle for the final time before resuming the last leg of their journey. "Get back on the perch, where you belong, Jocko," Nicky growled as he cracked his whip.

"I'm going, I'm going. No need to bite me 'ead off. I tell you again, guv, it ain't me as you needs worry about. Far as I'm concerned, from 'ere on out you're Major Wincanton as I ever knew 'im.''

When they approached the city, the sun made its first appearance of the day in the act of dipping low. It bathed the pale stone that gave Bath its distinction with a golden light. Nicholas pulled his grays to the roadside and shaded his eyes with his hand to drink in the scene. They focused first on the abbey tower, then moved on toward other church spires and chimney pots. The view was impressive, he had to admit. And ominous. Had Napoleon stood thus on the eve of battle and gazed at the fields of Waterloo?

"Thinkin' of turning tail, then, was you?"

Nicky gave the tiger a quelling look, then flicked the reins.

Reaching his destination posed no problem. He simply weaved his way toward the imposing crescent that was clearly visible on Lansdown Hill. And when he drew alongside the elegant, curving row of houses, it seemed just one more circumstance put there to daunt him that of all the dwellings that comprised the Lansdown Crescent, Number Twenty was the most imposing of the lot. Lady Stoke's residence was situated on the west end of the crescent, with a five-storied elevation and a semicircular bow to distinguish its facade.

Jocko jumped from the curricle to hold the horses, and

Nicky pointedly ignored the impish grin as he climbed down stiffly from the driver's seat. As he headed for the entryway, which led to a side lane, his newly acquired limp was rather more pronounced than the one the bona fide major's stiff knee usually produced.

"Other leg, guv!" the tiger hissed behind him.

Nicky turned in consternation, to find Jocko convulsed.

"Just funnin', guv!" he mouthed while Nicky made a firm and solemn vow to horsewhip the rascal at the earliest opportunity.

"Major Wincanton to see Lady Stoke."

Well, that had sounded authoritative enough, and the starchy butler hadn't turned a hair. In fact, there was exactly the proper note of deference in the majordomo's "Come in, sir" and in his manner as he relieved Nicky of his beaver and greatcoat. "I'll tell her ladyship you're here, sir." The butler ushered the caller into a very modern withdrawing room.

Though the room was actually quite large, it did not initially seem so, for it was cluttered with a profusion of furniture that had been placed in helter-skelter fashion with no attempt at any formal arrangement. At least that was Nicky's first impression, and he found himself at a loss among such an array of choices when bidden to sit down. Chairs, sofas, settees, couches, stools, abounded, seemingly abandoned on the spot by exhausted movers. Candle stands, sconces, all sorts of tables, were scattered here and there. A pianoforte graced one end of the room; a harp, another. And everywhere he looked he discovered what he dismissed as bric-a-brac but what actually translated into vases, urns, china jars, candlesticks, busts, snuffboxes—an infinite variety of objets d'art worth a considerable fortune.

There was some method to the madness, though, he

finally concluded as he chose one of the chairs placed near a rosewood-inlaid table awash with books. The plan would be, Sit here if you wished to read. And there were other groupings, it appeared, for music of each type and for conversation.

Nicky picked up a leather-bound volume from the table and examined it, hoping to divert his mounting panic. *Mysterious Warnings*, the gilded title read. He took it as an omen and almost bolted.

"Gareth Wincanton! I don't believe it! Can it really, actually be you?"

Oh, dear God, unmasked already! Nicky rose unsteadily to his feet and turned to face the door. A plump, pleasant-looking lady who was past her middle years but certainly not the relic he'd expected stood on the threshold, looking him up and down. Her baby-blue eyes widened with surprise, and he held his breath. "Why, Gareth"—she came sailing toward him—"you quite took my breath away. Who'd have believed that such an unpromising and, frankly, quite horrid little boy, not to mention a Wincanton of any stripe, could have actually turned into an Adonis!

"Why, my dear, you're actually blushing! 'Struth—your face is every bit as red as your delightful hair. Bless me, but I find that charming." Her ladyship extended a beringed hand to be kissed. Nicky was happy to linger over it in order to pull himself together once again.

"Do come sit back down, Gareth dear," she said as she reluctantly retrieved her hand. "I may call you, Gareth, may I not? But of course—what a foolish question. I am your auntie, after all. By marriage only, though. And in truth I do feel rather odd about the relationship, if you'll forgive my saying so. Your uncle was much, much older than I, you see."

"That explains it. For, to be honest, I had not expected such a youthful aunt." Nicky managed the required gallantry with ease, since it was literal truth. "And please call me Win, if you don't object to such informality," he added as she beamed at him across the table. "My friends all do."

"Then Win it shall be. I much prefer it to Gareth. Whatever possessed your parents to give you such an outlandish name? And you must address me as Louisa. I refuse to be called 'aunt' by the handsomest man in Bath—especially since I've no real claim to the relationship.

"But oh, do forgive me, m'dear. Here I am, prattling on, and you must be famished. We had early dinner, but I'll ring for a cold collation. And oh, my heavens, what an addlepate you must think me! Has Hope seen to your baggage yet?"

Nicky made a protesting murmur about not wishing to impose and declared his intention of putting up at the White Hart. But as the major had prophesied, her ladyship was scandalized by the mere suggestion. "Of course you'll stay here." She spoke with finality. "Put Major Wincanton in the blue room, Hope," she ordered as the butler appeared in answer to her ring.

"I've already seen to the major's things, m'lady, as well as to his equipage and his, er, groom." The butler, who had been forewarned by her ladyship of a possible visit from her nephew, seemed awesome in his efficiency. His employer merely nodded, unsurprised. "And bring a supper tray in here, Hope. The dining room's so cold and formal," she confided to her visitor. "No place to get acquainted. And while you're eating, I'd like us to be able to have a comfortable coze."

Even though he'd just realized he hadn't had a bite since

Amabel's makeshift breakfast, this prospect routed Nicky's emerging appetite. But when the simple repast of cold partridges, oysters, hare, glazed neat's tongue, accompanied by a host of side dishes, was set before him, along with a decanter of port and the promise of coffee and chocolates to follow, in spite of his impending doom he set to work with a will.

And as he ate, his hostess talked. He had expected an inquisition. He got a monologue. She filled him in on Bath society—or the lack of it. On the entertainment to be found there—or the dearth of it. And went on to expound on the theme that now that the fates had accorded her a double blessing—his arrival and the fact that one of her oldest, dearest friends had just taken up residence in the Royal Crescent—all the aspersions she had formerly cast on Bath were now just so many words she'd be forced to eat. For with the handsome Major Wincanton and the distinguished Sir George Carstairs among its company, Bath was sure to become the most delightful of places. "Why, it will not surprise me in the least if the Prince Regent gets wind of our gaiety and abandons Brighton to build himself a new pavilion at Bath.

"But oh, goodness, what a rattle you must think me. I haven't allowed you the chance to get in a word. Tell me. How have you been spending your time in London?"

Then, before Nicky could swallow the mouthful he was chewing—he must remember: bad ton to take such bites—Lady Stoke had gotten a second wind and was well and truly launched into a satirical description of the various types who flocked to the Pump Room at set times of the day to drink their prescribed courses of the waters there.

Nicky was only thankful for her garrulousness. It never occurred to him as he ate his steady way through the repast that her chatter covered a nervousness almost equal to his and gave her opportunity to consider just what tack to take. By the time he'd reached the coffee stage and she'd poured out for both of them, Lady Stoke had made up her mind.

"I do believe that in the long run honesty is much the best policy, don't you?"

He'd just taken a large gulp of the steaming liquid and strangled on it. "I beg your pardon?" he managed to gasp when he'd recovered from his fit.

"It's what that Franklin fellow wrote. At least I believe he was the one. You know, that American chap with all those tedious sayings. Or was it Aesop? Well, never mind all that. It was one of those prosy types, at any rate, and in this case I expect that whoever said it was dead right. Honesty usually is the best policy. Don't you agree?"

He nodded dumbly, turning pale.

"Well, so do I, and I collect I'd best be candid in this instance and make a clean breast of the situation. For now that I've met you, I'm certain that you'll be all understanding and realize that what I'm going to say is in the best interests of all concerned and can in no way be taken as idle gossip-mongering."

He was still frozen at the moment of realization that *she* was the one who was supposed to make a clean breast of things, and had taken nothing in beyond that point. But he saw that her eyes were fixed upon him expectantly and felt obliged to utter. "I don't quite understand," he managed to say.

"I know you don't, dear," she replied kindly. For Lady Stoke had just concluded that although the major outstripped the rest of the Wincantons as far as looks were concerned, he lagged somewhat behind that family's average for intellect. "I haven't gotten around yet to explaining. But the more I think of it, the more convinced I become that it's the thing to do. That tedious man was right—that is, if he was the one to say it—honesty is the best policy after all, and you will keep everything I say in the strictest confidence, will you not? I wouldn't wish her to know I'd been so forthcoming. But how else can I get your cooperation?''

Again she paused expectantly. But Nicky was remembering Major Wincanton's dictum ''When you don't know the proper thing to say, for God's sake keep your mouth closed.'' It seemed to apply to the present moment. Indeed, Nicky began to fear he might be forced into perpetual muteness.

Lady Stoke's mind had been diverted, however, from ethical considerations to more immediate ones. ''Oh, my goodness, I hadn't thought. Here I'd simply taken it for granted that you yourself—so recently back from the Continent and all—must be unattached. Tell me, Win. Do you have an understanding with anyone?''

''An understanding? Am I betrothed, you mean? Oh, lord, no. Nothing like that, I assure you.''

''Good. That *would* be unfortunate.''

It could have been, however, that Lady Stoke picked up on some insincerity in his answer, for she was moved to probe a little deeper. ''A tendre, then? A man like you must be constantly falling in love. Is there a particular young lady who has perhaps already fixed your interest?''

''No.'' Again that bit of hesitation. ''There's no young . . . lady.''

''Well, then I'm much relieved to hear it. A man in love is so . . . so . . . unobjective. And I need you to tell me what's to be done in a certain situation.''

''And just what situation is that, Lady—er, I mean to say, Louisa?'' Nicky asked with mounting apprehension.

''Well, you see, my boy, you are not my only visitor.

49

Although in her case 'visitor' is not what the French call the mot juste. What I fear I have acquired is a companion. Which is the last thing in the world I ever wanted. You've no idea of how awkward it is to have someone always under foot. And now especially, with Porge living in Bath. I've no privacy at all to— Alas, the young are so censorious. Don't you agree? But how absurd!'' She laughed. ''I'm speaking as if you were of my age, instead of a mere lad. But then, you're a man of the world, Win. Not to be compared with—

''But goodness, how selfish you must think me. I vow it's not my own interests I'm most concerned with. For it's very lowering, I tell you, to see someone one really cares for fossilize before one's very eyes when there's a world of dances and assemblies and plays and concerts and routs and all the rest out there just waiting to be enjoyed, though perhaps not in Bath. But anyhow, Win dear, that's where you come in. And why it's such a very fortunate coincidence that you should have unexpectedly taken the notion to come here. Oh, my heavens!'' She broke off in consternation at the sound of rapidly approaching footsteps. ''We must not be caught discussing—'' she whispered conspiratorially. ''Quick! Speak of something else!''

''Yes. Ah. Hmmm. Oh, well, yes, do tell me, Lady Stoke, how is the theater here?''

Nicky savagely cursed himself for reverting to type. He'd completely lost his Wincanton character, if indeed he'd ever had it.

But Lady Stoke did not seem to find the question odd. Indeed, she picked up on it gratefully. ''Ah, the theater! I'm so glad you asked.'' She spoke in animated, carrying tones. ''For that's one feature of Bath society that we need not blush for.'' She turned from him and smiled as a young lady wearing a dark violet pelisse and bonnet hurried into the room. "Ah, Venetia, my dear!"

"I'm back, Aunt Louisa. I did not wish to worry you, but— Oh, I am sorry. I did not realize you have a caller."

Nicky rose slowly to his feet, trying valiantly to appear debonair and nonchalant, while feeling like a trapped fox with the hound pack circling. Who the devil was this female? And why hadn't he been told about her?

He found himself being coolly appraised by a pair of beautiful dark eyes that seemed to see right through him. And the owner of the stare, with her cheeks flushed pink from walking in the cold and her blond curls wind-blown where they peeped from underneath her modish bonnet, quite took his breath away and called to mind vague recollections of statuary he'd once seen of young Greek goddesses. Not, perhaps, that this newcomer quite possessed a classic beauty. It was her aristocratic mien, no doubt, that caused her to appear Olympian and placed her high above mere mortals like himself.

"This is no ordinary caller, Venetia dear," Lady Stoke was saying with a heartiness that sounded artificial even to Nicky Forbes's benumbed ears. "Win here has actually torn himself away from the delights of the metropolis to keep his auntie company for a while. But heavens, what can I be thinking of? I'd forgotten you two have never actually met. Venetia, pray allow me to present my nephew, Major Gareth Wincanton, who has just returned to this country after ridding the world of that Corsican monster. And this, Win dear, is my niece, Lady Venetia Lowther."

"Charmed," Nicky murmured as he bent low over the goddess's hand. "I'd no idea," he continued with perfect truth, "that I even possessed such a lovely cousin "

He glanced up at the sound of a disdainful sniff. The young lady's eyes were no longer appraising. They had come to judgment. And the look he was impaled with was disbelieving, scornful, and, above all else, hostile.

Chapter
Five

*M*ajor Wincanton's *eyes were glued upon the stage,* but his mind was miles away in Bath and centered upon Nicky Forbes. Unconsciously he grimaced with distaste.

He had lately begun to develop an acute dislike of the actor after an initial impression that had been quite favorable. As an officer, Win had had opportunity to assess Forbes the soldier and had found him quick-witted and courageous, though inclined to shirk responsibility whenever possible. But Private Forbes's chief claim to fame, the major now recalled, was as a womanizer. He'd been a menace to the female population for the length and breadth of the Iberian peninsula.

It was this aspect of the other's character that Wincanton was inclined to dwell on as he sat in his box at Drury Lane while the plot of *The Fatal Marriage* unfolded. He had no need to follow the action. He'd seen the production a score of times before and could, if pressed, recite great chunks of the dialogue himself. He vowed every day not to return to the theater that night and found himself every evening once again ensconced in the stage box. But at least he felt no compunction to follow the progress of the drama except for those electrifying times when Miss Fawnhope appeared onstage. But since she was not there at this moment, he was at complete liberty to follow the direction of his thoughts. And perversely they returned again and again to Nicky Forbes.

It wasn't enough that Wincanton was concerned with the shambles the actor was no doubt making of his reputation. What really was galling to contemplate was a fact that he'd lately been forced to acknowledge: he, Major Gareth Wincanton, officer and aristocrat, was actually jealous of a common soldier. A Cit, no less. An actor, to boot. And a god-awful actor at that.

The acknowledgment of this degrading emotion was an enormous blow to Wincanton's considerable pride. But he was far too honest to pretend that the jealousy did not exist or to avoid analyzing the cause of it.

For one thing, he resented all the constant references to a nonexistent physical resemblance. Oh, he'd grant the hair. But why make so much of it? If they'd both had brown or blond hair, no one would comment. And outside of that one attribute, he could see little basis for the comparison.

He was convinced that his irritation with the subject of their looks had nothing to do with the fact that the actor held the edge. Wincanton had no desire for handsomeness.

Let Forbes have that asset for the stage. God knew he needed all the help that he could get. No, the plain truth was, it galled him to be look-alike to a member of the lower class. And why so many people insisted on making the comparison was a mystery. Even Amabel had done so. On more than one occasion.

That was it, of course. Therein lay the rub. Major Wincanton had not built his distinguished military career upon false assessments. He was able to look a fact directly in the face, no matter how distasteful it might be. And his growing dislike of Mr. Nicholas Forbes, he now acknowledged, was based almost in its entirety upon the actor's relationship with Miss Fawnhope.

When the actress had first presented her ''brother'' to him, he'd been pleased to recognize a fellow veteran of the Napoleonic Wars. Besides, he badly needed an ally in the siege he was laying against Miss Fawnhope's unexpectedly strong defenses. Her own brother was the very ticket. And the ex-private seemed more than willing—eager, in fact—to whisper into his sister's ear a good word on his ex-major's behalf.

But little by little, as he recalled his relationship with his own sisters, Wincanton began to wonder whether Nicholas and Amabel weren't too close by half. And he'd discovered after a bit of inquiry that the two were no blood kin at all. In fact, they had no claim even to an in-law relationship, since their parents hadn't bothered to legalize their liaison.

It was at this point that the green-eyed monster had made its appearance and Wincanton had begun to wonder just what sort of game the ''brother-sister'' team was playing. Certainly if Nicholas was pleading his major's case the way he claimed to be, there'd been no results of this advocacy so far. Wincanton found that fact suspicious. For he had no doubt at all of the actor's influence on his "little sister." Sometimes the major felt she could talk of nothing else. It was "Nicky this" and "Nicky that" till he was ready to grind his teeth at the very sound of the other's name.

No, Win thought as he stared blankly toward the stage, he'd found no ally in the former Private Forbes. Why he'd ever trusted the scoundrel was past all understanding. He had no doubt now that the two were in collusion against him, playing deep. Well, if they thought they could maneuver him into marriage, they were due a rude awakening. Or any long-term commitment, when it came to that. He'd cut his eyeteeth long ago and was not about to be taken in by any bit of muslin, no matter how lusciously appealing. The major smiled sardonically to himself. But just then Miss Fawnhope made her entrance, to the sound of wild applause, and Wincanton felt his pulses begin to race while at the same time all his resolution melted.

"You're very quiet, sir." Three hours later Amabel Fawnhope gave Wincanton a searching look as she nibbled at a chicken wing. She had worked her way ravenously through sweetbreads, lobster patties, tongue with cauliflower; now her hunger was sated enough for her to notice his unusual silence and lack of appetite. "And you've eaten nothing."

'No, I'm not hungry."

He never failed to be astounded at the amount of provision the sylphlike Miss Fawnhope managed to put away without any noticeable damage to her alluring figure. He did, however, wonder just how much longer such a happy state of affairs could go on. Once, when she'd seen his eyes widen as she ate, she'd explained that acting required an enormous output of energy and left her famished. But it still occurred to him now and then that she had possibly passed beyond the bounds of ladylike behavior.

"Blue-deviled?" she inquired as she put the chicken bone upon her plate and licked her fingertips daintily with her enticing tongue. "Or are you still pouting over coming here?"

"I never pout." He smiled as he reached for the iced champagne and filled both their glasses.

There had been a time when he'd had high hopes for that particular potable, expecting it to soften Amabel's resistance. Now he knew that the actress would always stop well short of intoxication. He could do worse, he reminded himself, than to profit by her example. He felt a keen desire to get roaring drunk but recalled only too well the penalty for that particular overindulgence.

"And even if I were subject to pouting fits," he continued, "a most unmanly—not even to mention unsoldierly—pursuit, I'd certainly not indulge myself because of an argument we've had every evening since I've met you. Don't I always extend a gracious invitation to you to visit my rooms, where, believe me, the hospitality is far superior to this?" His scornful look took in the appointments of the private parlor he'd engaged in the Hummums Hotel and the remains of the repast she'd been enjoying. "And don't you always refuse?"

"Yes, because we both know just what that hospitality would include, don't we?"

"It would include a supper prepared by the finest cook, bar none, in London. Wine far superior to this pap we're drinking. And as to what other, er, *diversions* the evening might provide, well, that would be entirely up to you. I am, after all, a gentleman."

"And gentlemen never lose their heads, I suppose?"

"Gentlemen never force ladies to do anything against their wills."

"Oh, well, then. There you have it. It's my own weak nature that I must guard against. You're a very attractive, persuasive man, Major Wincanton, so I collect it's best to stay with the inferior, but far safer, hospitality of the Hummums."

"Do you know, Amabel"—he gazed at her thoughtfully as he twirled the crystal stem of his wineglass between his fingers—"I think you're developing into a deliberate tease."

"And I deny it." She tossed her head. "Teasing has nothing to say in the matter. I'm not one of your highborn ladies, Gareth, with all sorts of social conventions set up to guard my reputation. I'm an actress. Which means I have little enough reputation to begin with. But I value what I have. The problem is that I do want your company. You've quite turned my head, in fact. I've deserted all my old friends just to be with you. But I am not prepared, Win darling, to throw my cap over the windmill for you. Or for any man."

He believed about half of what she was saying. She'd resisted all his attempts to bed her, and he'd begun to recognize that she had no intention of ever weakening. It was the latter part of her declaration that he doubted. It was difficult—if not impossible—for him to believe in an actress's chastity. True, there'd been no rumors about Amabel, and, God forgive him, he'd made inquiries. But now that her "brother," Nicky, had come back into her life, well, who knew what went on in that free and easy—and intimate—relationship? Just the thought of it put Wincanton's blood on the boil. For some absurd reason, he felt cuckolded.

Even as she changed the subject to chat of this and that,

underneath her easy manner Amabel was also doing some serious thinking. She was more concerned over Wincanton than she planned to show. She had not seen him like this before. He had avoided her for two whole days and nights. And now that he'd picked up where they'd left off, he seemed entirely different.

Was there someone else, perhaps? Amabel was well acquainted with the fickleness of the other sex. Still, some instinct told her his obsession had not waned. She began to have uneasy second thoughts about her campaign tactics.

As if he read her mind, Wincanton said abruptly, "I can't marry you, you know, Amabel. That's out of the question."

Those who thought Miss Fawnhope had reached her leading-lady status on the boards simply by her beauty much mistook the matter. She was an actress and thus was able to suppress her true reaction to that flat, bald statement and substitute one more appropriate to her purposes. "Of course not." She smiled enchantingly. "The idea's unthinkable. Why, what would your dear mama say?"

In spite of knowing she was being deliberately provocative, he was nettled. "My mother's reaction has little to say in the matter. It's the polite world in general I'm concerned with."

"I know you are, Gareth." She dropped her teasing manner and was suddenly all seriousness. "Society's opinion is all-important to you. Which goes to prove one thing: you don't love me. If you did, you wouldn't care a fig what anyone thought about a misalliance."

She paused, waiting, perhaps, for him to deny what she'd just said. But in all honesty he couldn't. She smiled once more, this time with a trace of bitterness. "So it seems we've reached a stalemate. Is that the right term, Win?''

"It will do."

"You do understand, of course, why I cannot give you what you wish." When he merely shrugged without answering, she chided him gently, "Well, you ought to understand. And even if you do not, since my refusal only affects your vanity and not your heart it's really a small matter after all. There are plenty of other girls prettier than I who would be more than happy to satisfy your . . . appetite. And if my refusal to do so pricks your self-esteem, well, I've told you time and time again that it should not do so." Her gaze was melting as she met his eyes across the table and held them. Her voice was low and husky. "For I've told you time and time again that I find you—almost— irresistible. And if there were any man at all that I was willing to live in sin with, well, it would be you."

It was a touching moment. The look she gave him was wistful, longing, tinged with regret, and almost convincing. Damn her lying little heart, he thought viciously. Why did I ever involve myself with an actress, anyway?

Amabel sighed at his continued silence. "That was intended to salve your pride, Gareth. Which, as I've just said, is the only emotion of yours involved. Come now." She reached a hand across the table and covered his. "Can't we still be friends?"

He shook off the hand as though it burned him. "No, Amabel, we cannot be friends. I don't want you for a friend. I'm well supplied with friends. Thank you all the same." He rose abruptly. "Come on. I'll take you home."

They walked the short distance to her house in silence, ignoring the crowded gin shops they passed and the ladies of the evening casting out their lures to the rash young bloods out for a night of adventure. Amabel's mind was racing furiously. What happened next was crucial if she hoped to keep him dangling after her. When they reached her door, she turned to gaze up at him. Her face, in the glow of a nearby street lamp, was tortured. "It's just as well that I can't ask you in tonight," she whispered.

"Since you never have, I'll hardly notice the omission."

"But I've explained all that. Nellie insists on waiting up for me. She's like a second mother. Watches me like a hawk."

In all likelihood, of course, Nellie was at the Queen's Head Tavern, swilling gin with her cronies. Amabel only hoped she wouldn't come reeling around the corner before the major left.

"But as I was saying, it's just as well that I can't be tempted to ask you inside, for I've come to a dreadfully difficult decision. I don't think we should see each other anymore."

"It does seem rather pointless."

Although this certainly was not the cue she'd expected, Miss Fawnhope, the trooper, did not muff her mentally rehearsed lines. "That's too true. And for me, well, our association has grown far, far too painful. Frankly, Gareth darling, I don't know how much longer I can find the strength to hold out against you. So it's time we drew apart. Good-bye, my dearest. Pray, do not forget me."

Tears spilled down her face as the little actress rose on tiptoe to place her lips on his.

The kiss was long and passionate. She pressed her body provocatively against him. Then, when inevitably his lips and hands began to wander, she allowed them liberties they'd never enjoyed before. But just as he'd begun to entertain thoughts of dragging her off behind the shrubbery, Amabel wrenched herself free of his embrace and leaned, gasping, against the door. "Oh, you do see what I mean, Gareth love. This *has* to be good-bye." And before he could get his own hard breathing under control to answer her, she'd eased through her door and shut it in his face.

Major Gareth Wincanton stood glaring at the oak portal for a moment, then turned and walked unsteadily away, his limp far more pronounced than usual. He was cursing fluently underneath his breath. And his oaths were all directed at one source—the beautiful, provocative, unscrupulous Miss Amabel Fawnhope.

For the major had no illusions about the scene that had just been enacted. "The little trollop's hooked me well and proper," he muttered viciously to himself, "and now, by God, she's playing me like a fish."

Chapter
Six

When Nicholas Forbes crossed the threshold of the breakfast parlor and realized that Lady Venetia Lowther was its sole occupant, he almost beat a hasty, ignominious retreat. But before he could suit action to the impulse, she glanced up from the boiled egg she was cracking and bent a smile upon him that was as cordial as it was unexpected.

Nicholas had spent a fretful night tossing and turning on his fine linen sheets and—despite the fact that he'd landed in more luxury than he ever knew existed—wishing himself almost anywhere, up to and including the fields of Waterloo, than where he was. And the chief reason for his unease was Lady Venetia Lowther.

In the first place, her ladyship had been completely omitted from his briefing. Nicky still didn't know just who the devil she was. His initial stab at establishing the creature's identity had brought on her hostile atmosphere and a "Don't be ridiculous, Win dear—you know she's not your cousin" from Louisa. After that, they had settled in for what proved to be a most uncomfortable half hour of stilted conversation while Lady Venetia continued to look daggers at both Nicky and her aunt. This awkward interval had been terminated by the arrival of a Sir George Carstairs (another member of the dramatis personae the major's tutoring had omitted) dressed in evening clothes to collect Lady Stoke for a party that she had forgotten completely.

It was suggested that Lady Venetia and the major accompany them. The former icily pleaded the headache and withdrew, while the latter claimed fatigue as his reason for forgoing the proffered entertainment. There was no civil way, however, that he could have avoided keeping Sir George company while Lady Stoke hurried off to change.

But all in all that tête-à-tête hadn't gone too badly. Sir George showed no inclination to doubt his bona fides. And like his lady friend, the elderly gentleman seemed perfectly content to carry the lion's share of the conversation. When he did at last get around to probing for mutual acquaintances, Nicky was able to come up with "Sprig" St. Leger, whom they spent some time discussing. After that, Sir George seemed content to attribute any apparent memory lapses to the major's long absence on the Continent.

So Nicky felt that on the whole he had acquitted himself quite well in that encounter. Then, when a rather breathless Lady Stoke entered the withdrawing room, wearing a crimson crepe evening gown and a toplofty headdress of matching ostrich feathers, there was no time for more than her thrice-repeated apology for deserting her guest so soon after his arrival—"If it were anyone else but that odious Countess De Wint giving the party, I'd cry off. But she's bound to take offense, which would never do"—and a whispered aside after she'd proffered a cheek for him to kiss: "Never mind about Venetia, dear. I'd meant to prepare you for her. She'll come around. Though it may take a while."

Well, judging from the way Lady Venetia sat at her breakfast, smiling his way, she had done just that. And in record time. Nicky looked at her ladyship warily.

"Oh, do come get your breakfast, Major Wincanton. I won't eat you. In fact, I've been framing what I trust will be a handsome apology."

Even with that heartening forecast, Nicky still had little appetite as he looked over the array that crowded the sideboard. He settled on ham, rolls, butter, and chocolate and carried his plate over to the table, where he resisted the impulse to distance himself as far from her ladyship as the breakfast table would allow and, instead, sat down beside her. He took a sip of the chocolate and studied her covertly.

He was able to reestablish the impression he had made upon first seeing her, before her hostility had made him think of harridans and harpies. Lady Venetia was a very attractive woman. Indeed, were she less elevated in station and were he the same old Nicky Forbes as ever was, he couldn't have asked for a more desirable breakfast companion. But she wasn't and he wasn't, and he did wish his stomach would unknot and that he knew just what the devil was going on.

"You must have thought me rude past all redemption when we met last evening," she remarked.

He was pleased to note that she actually sounded embarrassed. It made her almost human. His stomach un-knotted one small notch.

"Well," he answered tentatively, "I must admit to be-ing a trifle puzzled by your attitude. People usually have to know me a great deal better to dislike me all that much." He produced a crooked, charming smile, and she laughed spontaneously.

"Believe me when I say it was nothing personal. Or, at least, in a manner of speaking it was not. I merely took exception to the reason for your being here. But after our aunt rang a peal over me and I had some time to think things over, I came to realize that was no excuse for being uncivil to you. Nor to Aunt Louisa. For exasperating as I find all her maneuvering, I do need to keep in mind that she's only acting from the kindest of motives— Oh, my goodness!" She broke off suddenly. "I fear I'm beginning to sound just like Aunt Louisa!"

"I must admit the both of you tend to make the head spin, if you'll pardon me for saying so."

"Well, then, I must try to regain the habit of plain speaking. Though too much candor is a particular vice of mine, I'm told. Goodness, there I go again! What I'm trying to say is that now that I've had time to cool down a bit, I realize how churlishly I behaved. And I have also come to realize that Aunt is right. Just because I've been burned once, I can't go on avoiding fire forever.

"Oh, dear, what a mull I'm making of all this. And after my brave declaration about plain speaking. But it *is* humiliating, as you must understand, to have Aunt Louisa out beating the bushes to find suitors for me. And it did seem the outside of enough that just when she'd given up on Bath and I thought I could relax a bit, she's begun to import gentlemen for me. But last night, in lieu of sleep-ing, I came to realize that the poor dear is not half so desperate on my account as on her own.'' She smiled a self-deprecating smile. ''She wants me off her hands. And while I'd like nothing better than solitary independence, I realize that spinsters, for the most part, are barred from that sensible course of action. Therefore, I've resigned myself to the fact that I must marry. And so, Major Wincanton, I'm quite prepared to pretend that you're dangling after me for my beauty, wit, and charm and are not influenced in the slightest by my handsome fortune. Oh, my word! I say, are you all right?''

''Major Wincanton'' had strangled, sent his chocolate spraying across the table, and was now having a coughing fit. Venetia sprang up and thumped him between the shoulder blades till he finally subsided. ''Here, sip this slowly.'' She thrust a water goblet into his hand and resumed her seat.

''Oh, dear. I am sorry. As I said, I've been taken to task repeatedly about my odious habit of plain speaking. Fletcher was most eloquent on that point right after I'd told him just what I thought of his cozy little love nest. Proper females, he informed me, choose to overlook such unpleasantries. So I am aware that a lady should always believe she's being pursued for herself alone. But I don't seem to have the knack of self-delusion. If you'll be patient with me, though, I'll try to cultivate it.''

Nicky's coughing had gradually subsided. As had his apprehension. For he'd come to realize that the charade he'd embarked upon was hopeless. Even if there were only Lady Stoke to fool, the situation would have been touch and go. But now, with this latest development, there was no way he could get by with the impersonation. His situation was far, far worse than the actor's nightmare of being onstage and forgetting his lines. Hell, he didn't even know what play they were doing! But along with despair came calm. He felt the sort of resignation he'd felt in battle. Since he was about to be annihilated anyhow, he'd go out with flair.

And so, for the first time, he looked at Lady Venetia as he might have looked at any garden-variety female—and lord knew he had plenty of experience with those types. "Just who the devil is Fletcher, and where did you get the maggoty notion that I'm interested in either you or your money?" he inquired. "I never even knew of your existence until last night. Oh, I'll take your word for it that you're worth a fortune, though just why you think that's something that should send me jumping through hoops eludes me. My God, woman, I'm a regular nabob myself."

Well, now, a gentleman, he supposed, would not have made that speech, but he'd certainly taken the wind out of her nibs's sails and caused her chin to drop. By Jupiter, he felt his appetite returning. He picked up his plate and walked back to the sideboard, where he piled it high. When he returned to his place, she continued to stare in amazement, he noted, but at least she had closed her mouth.

Lady Venetia watched in silence as he attacked his beef ribs. Then, after a bit, she seemed to make up her mind. "I don't think you do know why Aunt Louisa sent for you. She didn't tell you about me, did she?"

"*Nobody* told me about you. And Louisa didn't send for me. This visit was my parents' idea entirely. My father wrote a blistering letter about how ungrateful it appeared for me to have been back in England for weeks now without visiting my uncle's widow. I am his heir, as Papa reminded me. He also informed me that Louisa was feeling quite neglected."

"Well, I do see our aunt's fine Italian hand at work," Venetia observed shrewdly. "But I can also see that I've done you an injustice." Her face turned pink. "Heavens, what you must think of me! Tying one's garters in public doesn't begin to describe what I've just done."

Nicky was enjoying her discomfort as he chewed his beef bones slowly. "Well, it's a bit late to stand on points now, don't you agree? So let's back up a bit. Just who is Fletcher?"

"My fiancé. My ex-fiancé, that is. We—I—called off our engagement."

"I see. And this Fletcher fellow. What makes you so certain it was just your fortune he was interested in?" Nicky was sizing her up with the eye of a connoisseur. "It strikes me that you could have mistaken the matter."

She colored a bit more under his appreciative gaze. "Oh, no. There was not the slightest doubt on that score. You see, I discovered that he kept a mistress. Had done so since before I met him."

"But he planned to give her up to marry you, of course."

"That's what he said. Though I doubt he actually would have done so. I think he was quite in love with her. At any rate, I did not care to put the competition to the test."

"I see." He paused to mull that over. "And did you love him?"

"My, you are direct." She grimaced. "Do you know I can hardly believe we're having this conversation? But since it's a bit late for missishness at this point, no, I don't think I ever did love Fletcher. Oh, he quite turned my head at first with his attentiveness." The light tone of voice she tried to adopt rang the least bit false. "For he was very good-looking. And charming. An incorrigible deceiver." Here Nicky barely managed not to wince. "But as I've tried to explain to Aunt Louisa, it was my pride that suffered the greatest blow. But she still insists upon believing

I have a broken heart. Hence her desperate roundup of suitors.''

"Like getting right back up on a horse once it's thrown you, I collect.''

She laughed. "I wouldn't have put it just that way, but yes, I suppose I have been thrown.''

"Don't you think that you're just possibly blowing the whole thing out of proportion? Oh, perhaps not the mistress part,'' he quickly qualified as she bristled. "But the fortune thing. After all, there's nothing so unusual about that. Don't most of the people of your—*our* class marry for convenience? And there's nothing more convenient than a fortune.''

"Oh, you're right, of course. And Aunt is, too. I have far too many romantic notions for a female of my years. And so, during the wee hours of this morning, I decided that I'd turn over a brand-new leaf. I shall make myself as available as anyone could wish and accept the next 'convenient' offer that comes my way.''

She was gazing at him speculatively. He willed himself not to tug at his cravat, which all of a sudden felt quite constrictive. For after an all-too-short-lived reprieve, Nicholas Forbes was beginning to grow decidedly uneasy once again.

Chapter Seven

"*Oh, my! If you could see your face!*" Lady Venetia laughed across her teacup, while Nicky could only manage a sheepish grin. "I can assure you there's no need for panic. I haven't the slightest intention of setting my cap for *you*. And you must not allow Aunt Louisa to browbeat you on my behalf.

"But now that I think of it, you must be accustomed to having females thrown at your head, self-confessed nabob that you are."

"Actually, no. There was little opportunity for match-making where I've been."

"Of course. How stupid of me. When Aunt Louisa was raking me over the coals for being so rag-mannered, she did say you took part in the most dreadful part of the fighting and behaved most heroically."

This was a subject Nicky would have been quite happy to expand on, feeling more at home on the fields of Waterloo than in the muddied waters of their relationship. But she denied him that opportunity. "So you haven't had much chance, then, to be viewed as quite a catch. How long did you say you've been in London?"

"Six weeks."

"Oh, well, then, I was wrong. That's ample time for the debutantes at Almack's and their scheming mamas to besiege you. A fortune and handsome, too! You're far too valuable a prize to escape for long. La, I'm amazed they ever allowed you to leave town."

"Well, to tell the truth, I've never been to Almack's."

"You astound me! I know its exclusiveness is legendary, but I cannot believe you were denied admittance, given your pedigree *and* your nabobery."

"You're roasting me, ain't you? I daresay I should not have mentioned my wealth."

"Oh, indeed not. Frightfully bad ton."

"Well, you goaded me into it. Besides, you admitted to being an heiress."

"I know. I share the blame. But I can't believe that you've spent six weeks in London without visiting the most famous marriage mart in the kingdom. You really must be gun-shy. And to think that Aunt Louisa despairs of me!"

"I will admit I've little desire to become leg-shackled. At least, not yet." Whether speaking as Wincanton or himself, Nicky had no problem achieving the ring of conviction.

"Then we are well met, sir." Venetia's smile quite took his breath away. "So now that we know where we stand, can we not put Aunt Louisa in high gig by appearing to

72

fall in with her little scheme? Shall we begin this campaign immediately? Allow me to be your guide on a tour of Bath. I expect us to set the town agog.''

She excused herself to dress for their expedition. He sat at the breakfast table a little longer, seeking the fortification of two cups of tea while trying to assimilate this new turn of events.

A half hour later, they emerged from the Crescent. Lady Venetia was becomingly attired in a French gray walking dress ornamented with white lutestring, and Nicky looked most dapper in his brand-new maroon spencer jacket worn over a black tailcoat. She stopped short at the sight of a sporting curricle with a diminutive tiger who was suitably expressionless except for his lively, inquisitive eyes and who held the horses' heads. "Oh, dear. Is that your rig?" He nodded. "I had no notion that you'd ordered it. The day's so fine, I'd thought we'd walk. We can see so much more on foot. Oh!" She broke off in consternation. "I quite forgot. Your leg. How thoughtless of me. Of course we'll ride.''

"No, no. It's not at all necessary, I assure you. As a matter of fact, I'd much prefer to walk.''

There was no question of his sincerity. He disliked the thought of making conversation in front of Jocko Hodges. "Believe me, my leg seldom pains me at all.''

"That's right, m'lady," the irrepressible tiger chimed in. "Why, the major here can walk a treat when he's a mind to.

"Oh I say, *sir*"—he gave the title rather too much stress for Nicky's liking—"how about if I exercise these beasts just a bit before taking 'em back to the stables? Not to disappoint 'em, you might say." Jocko grinned impishly, looking forward to tooling through the town and turning the heads of pretty serving maids with his bang-up-to-the-nines equipage.

"Go ahead," Nicky answered, trying hard not to grind his teeth but looking forward to the day when he could connect the sole of his boot to the groom's derriere.

"What an odd little man," Venetia observed as the tiger sprang the horses. "Doesn't he seem rather overfamiliar?"

"A little, I suppose. But he's a dab hand with the cattle."

As they walked down Lansdown Hill, Nicky experimented with his limp, trying to reduce it to the minimum without abandoning it altogether. It had occurred to him that this mode of walking might wind up actually crippling him before they'd covered all the miles Venetia seemed to have in mind.

She noticed his erratic progress and asked anxiously, "Are you sure you're quite up to this?"

"Perfectly," he replied as he settled into a more rhythmic form of "dot and carry one." And noting the edge in his voice, Venetia judged it more tactful not to refer again to his infirmity.

She proved an excellent guide, new enough to Bath herself to find it interesting and charming. Also she was an indefatigable walker. Nicky was surprised to discover that athletic trait in a member of her class and sex.

They approached the heart of the city by way of the Royal Crescent, which she'd insisted he positively must see. And he was suitably impressed by the younger John Wood's masterpiece. Thirty houses of golden oolite stone were joined in a semiellipse, with Ionic columns supporting a continuous frieze. "It's magnificent, " Nicky pronounced as he limped past.

"Yes, isn't it. Aunt Louisa's friend Porge— Oh, my

heavens, I must not call him that. What I meant to say is Sir George Carstairs has just moved in there.''

Nicky barely restrained himself from asking what it might cost to live in such elegance. Instead, ''By the by,'' he asked, ''just what is his relationship with our mutual aunt?''

''Close, I assume,'' she gurgled. ''It's my suspicion, Major Wincanton—''

''Please, call me Win,'' he interrupted her. '' 'Major Wincanton' sounds so formal. After all, we are practically related.''

''Very well, then, *Win* it is. But to continue my gossip-mongering, I really do suspect that our mutual aunt, to use your term, has led a life best described as scandalous. No wonder she finds me so . . . dampening. And it's my guess that at one time Sir Porge was one of her— Oh, bother! I'm groping for some term that will sound halfway respectable.''

''Something in French, perhaps?''

''What a good idea. I'm sure they must have a perfectly marvelous word, if only I could think of it. They do have a flair for putting the best possible light on that sort of thing.''

''Yes, it's devilish hard to sound sinful in French, isn't it? The best the frogs can manage is attractive wickedness. But in plain English, I take it you're trying to tell me they were lovers.''

''Oh, I'm quite convinced of it. And though it really does seem improbable at their ages, I suspect they'd like to be again. Only Aunt is so well chaperoned. By me. Now have I scandalized you?''

''Quite the contrary. Considering their ages, I find the situation decidedly heartening. Something to look forward to, you could say.''

She giggled, then realized the conversation had strayed into quite improper channels. But she found it difficult to stand on points with this gentleman. For although they'd only just met, she'd rarely been as open with anyone as she had been with him in that astounding breakfast conversation. And she had enjoyed the openness. She looked up appreciatively at her tall companion and found his eyes fastened upon her with something of the same approval reflected in them. She hoped she wasn't blushing. The habit was too odiously missish by half.

Venetia reverted to her former role of tour guide. "Oh, here's the Circus. It was begun by the elder John Wood, then finished by his son." She and Nicky had been sauntering down Brock Street and were now approaching another monument to the Wood architectural genius. As the name implied, the Circus consisted of a complete circle of houses designed with three tiers of columns. And like the Royal Crescent, it was joined with one continuous frieze.

Recognizing his companion's need to shy away from their former intimacy, Nicky observed solemnly, "Look— they've used a different type of column for each story. I wonder why. Couldn't make up their minds among Doric, Ionic, and Corinthian, or just showing off their classical knowledge, do you suppose?"

"I think you're the one who's showing off. However did you happen to know a thing like that?"

"Oh, well, now, I'll admit I didn't learn a lot at school, but a few classical details did penetrate my skull and stay there." The "scholar," who had helped build the sets for various Greek tragedies in his adolescence, tried to look modest.

Venetia had begun to notice that the major's limp was

growing decidedly more pronounced and that there were tiny pain lines around his eyes.

The condition was brought on not by applied techniques of acting but from the fact that the genuine major had insisted that Nicky take his new Hessian boots, since there was not time enough to have some quality footwear made to the actor's measure. These were rubbing a blister on his heel.

Venetia was much concerned and tactfully steered them toward Milsom Street, insisting that she must rest a bit and that he, despite his ample and recent breakfast, could not remain in Bath one moment longer without visiting Molland's Pastry Cook Shop and sampling the buns the town was famous for.

And it was while his mouth was crammed with this delectable pastry that Nicky realized he'd become the subject of an intense scrutiny. A tall, ramrod-straight elderly man of distinguished, albeit flashy, appearance was staring at him from across the patron-filled room.

Oh, God, no! Nicky quickly averted his eyes and appeared to be listening with absorbed interest to his companion's description of other Bath treats held in reserve, to be produced like rabbits from a hat during the remainder of his visit. Meanwhile, out of the corner of his eye he watched the gray-haired man begin to move implacably his way.

"Nicky! Nicky, lad! Can it really be? Why, I'd no idea you were in Bath. Heard you were in the army. Well met! Well met, me boy!"

The rolling, pear-shaped tones caused all heads to turn their way as the gentleman proffered a hand, which Nicky stared at as though it were a cobra. He pushed his chair back from the small table he and Lady Venetia shared and rose to stand slightly behind his companion.

"I think you must have mistaken me for someone else, sir," he observed frigidly while he tried to convey with his facial expression that he much preferred not to be recognized.

His pantomime served only to bewilder the old actor, who had been in a touring company with Nicky's mother before his talents had taken him on to better things. "Why, aren't you young Nicholas Forbes?" he inquired. He looked to Lady Venetia for possible assistance and became more mystified than ever by her obviously well-born appearance. "But oh, dear, how embarrassing!" He at last picked up on Nicky's frantic if mystifying signaling. "Pray, do forgive me, sir, for this unpardonable intrusion. I mistook you for an old acquaintance, you see. Quite silly of me, for now that I see you closer, there's not the slightest resemblance between you and my old friend. Vanity!" He smiled with a charm capable of enveloping an entire theater. "Blame this intrusion upon the vanity that forbids me to wear my spectacles in public. Your servant, sir, madam." He bowed gracefully in their direction and withdrew while Nicky sank back weakly into his chair, hoping Venetia wouldn't notice that he'd broken out in a cold sweat. But since her eyes were following the actor's back as he left the pastry shop, Nicky was able to blot his forehead surreptitiously with his handkerchief before she turned to look at him.

"How very odd," she observed. "He seemed so sure at first that he knew you."

"It's not really all that odd." Nicky managed to sound quite nonchalant. "In fact, it's always happening to me—being mistaken for some other cove."

"Really?" She looked surprised. "I can't imagine why. I'd say your appearance is quite uncommon. Distinguished, one might say."

"Thank you." He smiled disarmingly. "It's the hair, you see. When you have a carroty mane like mine, you find that people tend to focus upon it to the exclusion of all else. At first, at any rate. I fear it's the fate of red-headed people to be interchangeable."

She laughed. "Yes, I can see how that might happen. But do you know who I believe that was?"

"Haven't the slightest notion," he lied.

"I'm sure it's Mr. Powell, the actor. He's appearing on stage here as King Claudius. I haven't seen this *Hamlet* yet, but I've heard it's very well done indeed. Yes, I'm almost sure that was Mr. Powell. Aunt Louisa pointed him out to me in the Pump Room soon after the play opened. We really must go see it, Win. They tell me that the performances at the Theatre Royal are every bit as good as those in London." She grew enthusiastic. "Yes, I'm quite determined to become a theatergoer again as a part of my social redemption. Come now, sir. I've put you squarely on the spot. As a gentleman you've no recourse except to say that it will be your greatest pleasure to escort me."

"It will be my greatest pleasure to escort you." Nicky spoke with apparent sincerity while inwardly he vowed at all costs to forgo that particular treat. The acting fraternity was not really that large. And even given his long absence from England, who was to say who else among the performers and stagehands might see and recognize him?

The encounter with the elderly actor had left him shaken. While he was fairly confident that Venetia's suspicions had not been aroused by it, another case or two of "mistaken identity" and the fat would well and truly be in the fire. The vision of Brooks' betting book came back once more to haunt him. If he lost the wager, he was ruined. The acting fee Wincanton was paying for this impersonation wouldn't cover even a fraction of his indebtedness.

"I beg your pardon?" He came back to the present, vaguely aware that Venetia had just addressed him and was waiting for a reply.

"Goodness, you were off woolgathering. I've just asked if we shouldn't plan a theater party with Aunt Louisa and Porge."

"Capital idea!"

"I was going to suggest that we go this Wednesday. But I suppose I should leave that up to Aunt Louisa to decide. Or do you have a preference?"

"No, no. Any evening you fix on will be all right with me."

And it would be, at that. For no matter which night they settled upon, that would be the evening when Major Wincanton's old war wound would become so excruciatingly painful that the veteran would have no choice except to forgo the promised theatrical treat and take groaningly to his bed.

Chapter
Eight

Major Gareth Wincanton was in the blackest of black moods. This interval in his life, between soldiering and settling down to the serious business of civilian living, was intended to be carefree. It was turning out to be anything but that.

He lay in bed in the middle of the morning, puffing on a cigar and thinking of the coil he'd become involved in. The actor had been impersonating him in Bath for over a week now. He'd had no word from Jocko Hodges, so he assumed that Forbes had not yet been unmasked. The first few hours should have been most crucial. How could that fifth-rate actor have managed it? His Aunt Louisa must have really reached her dotage to believe that jackanapes was the outcome of centuries of breeding and the acquired polish of England's finest public schools.

And then, inevitably, his thoughts moved on to the cause of all this curst tomfoolery. Miss Amabel Fawnhope! He puffed savagely on his cigar at the thought of that particular beauty. Clouds of smoke billowed underneath the brocade canopy, making the major's four-poster bed look like an illustration of the Great London Fire.

He had never been so outdone by any female. Their relationship was not a love affair; it was more like a military engagement, all tactics and maneuvers. And he, by God, was being outcampaigned by an amateur.

He thought back to the last time he had seen her, when she had led him on, only to shut the door firmly in his face. His counter to her blatant sexual teasing had been to fall back and regroup. Let the little baggage cool her heels awhile, he'd decided. Let her wonder if her fish had wriggled off the hook after all. So he'd spent the past few evenings in his club, willing himself not to succumb to the nagging desire that would have driven him to visit Drury Lane.

But his withdrawal, by all reports, was not having the desired effect. Instead of leaving the theater each evening dejected and alone, Miss Fawnhope, his friends had gleefully reported, had been squired by a different gentleman every night. Her bevy of admirers, quick to observe his absence, were queuing up, by God, to take his place.

The major viciously ground out his cigar. To think that he'd been worried about that old roué Sir Horace Leacock, with his wife and brood of children permanently in the country while he went whoring around the town. Amabel could handle the Leacocks of this world. Did the breed include him? the major wondered, but dismissed that disturbing thought as quickly as it had come. It was her latest swain that alarmed him. The one, he'd been told, who had stepped to the head of the line and claimed her hand for two evenings in a row—Lord Desmond Keating, fresh-faced and down from Oxford, a green one not yet dry behind the ears. Just the type to throw all caution to the winds and actually marry an ambitious young coquette if that was what she wanted.

If that was what she wanted! He flung the covers back and, shouting for his valet, got out of bed. Of course that was what she wanted! And any gudgeon of his class would do. All her talk of being in love with him was just so much moonshine. Well, the devil take little Miss Conniving Fawnhope!

The major was in a flaming temper all that day. His servants gave him as wide a berth as their duties would permit and, when together, discussed its possible cause. Some were inclined to believe his leg wound was bothering him. His limp, these observed, was more pronounced than usual. But the valet, who was a knowing one, shook his head sagaciously and intoned *"cherchez la femme,"* a foreign phrase that earned him the admiration of servants' hall.

It finally came as a great relief to the major's staff when, after slamming around his house in St. James's Square all day and merely toying with the sumptuous repast Cook had prepared for his dinner, he called for his evening clothes and went out. He did not, however, go to Drury Lane. Perversely, he told his driver to take him to Covent Garden Theatre instead.

The scene he observed when he arrived there was a familiar one. He'd seen others like it countless times before without remarking on it. It was the way of the world, that was all, and not such a bad way at that from his former perspective. Now he viewed through new eyes the numerous barques of frailty positioned strategically about the saloon, vying for the best advantage posts to cast out their lures. And his emotions varied. He felt revulsion at an old and raddled type compelled to cling to the game long after nature had declared her unfit; pity for an obviously frightened young ladybird, a child merely, who might have run away except for the gimlet-eyed madam watching like a hawk from across the room; and a fleeting erotic response to the smile of a provocative goddess dressed in a blue riding habit almost as brilliant as her eyes.

Later, as he composed a note to be carried from his box to the titian-haired opéra dancer he'd singled out in the burletta that was sandwiched between the tragedy and the farce, he thought of the tableau he'd witnessed in the saloon. He refused, though, to make comparisons between the commerce there and his own behavior.

Major Wincanton arrived at the Hummums Hotel around midnight with the beauty clinging like a limpet to his arm. It did not improve his disposition to discover that the private parlor, which he'd come to view as his own preserve, was preengaged. When the major took strong exception to this arrangement, the poor landlord was cast into a quake. The last thing he wished was to offend this wealthy member of the ton. But to preempt Lord Desmond Keating's arrangements was even more unthinkable.

And then, in one moment, it seemed that all the years devoted to being a genial host, to building up the type of clientele dear to any ambitious publican's heart, had become wasted, that indeed the entire edifice of the hotel was going to come crashing around his ears, when the young lordship in question came through the door with the lovely Miss Fawnhope's glove resting lightly upon his sleeve. For the landlord's greatest fear had become reality. Lord Desmond Keating had not only commandeered the major's parlor, but taken over his lady friend.

But the fireworks the innkeeper was braced for never happened, thanks entirely to the actions of Miss Fawnhope. For while the major continued to look like an impending storm and the noble calfling turned a trifle pale and the opera dancer looked quite confused, Miss Fawnhope broke into a dazzling smile. "Gareth!" she crooned. "How lovely to see you again. It's been ages. May I present Lord Desmond Keating? Oh, I see you've met. How nice." She paused expectantly, looking pointedly and pleasantly toward the beauty who was upon Wincanton's arm. Then, following a grudging introduction, she was cast into raptures by this chance meeting with a fellow artist, for she was dying to hear all the latest on-dits from Drury Lane's greatest rival; for instance, was it really so that Mr. Kemble was beside himself with jealousy over Mr. Kean?

When she suggested to his lordship that the foursome share the private parlor, the landlord wiped his brow and looked upon Miss Fawnhope as a female Solomon. But the major's curt refusal of this diplomatic gesture cast him back once more into nether gloom. Lord Desmond did not appear to share his host's dejection. Relief was writ large upon his face. The dancer, though, seemed disappointed, while Miss Fawnhope managed to look appealingly contrite.

"Oh, dear. What a perfectly goosish suggestion. What must I have been thinking? You two wish to be alone, of course. Pray, forgive me, Win."

Well, at any rate the crisis had been averted. The major accepted the landlord's second-best accommodation with a modicum of grace, and the host scurried off to the kitchen to make sure that the supper served would in all respects atone for any slight the major might have felt.

But only the opera dancer appreciated the feast laid out before them. She interspersed bites of lobster and sips of iced champagne with valiant attempts at conversation but got no help at all from Major Wincanton, who toyed with his food, his mind clearly elsewhere. When his wandering attention did occasionally return to her, it was to wonder why the devil he'd ever embarked upon this juvenile course to make Amabel Fawnhope jealous. The actress had seen right through him and was beating him soundly at his game. As for the dancer, he'd concluded that she was not nearly as stunning when seen up close as she'd appeared to be upon the stage. Too vapid by half, as well. The creature was, in fact, a bore.

And since the young woman was at least as disenchanted with her brilliant catch, there was relief all around when at the conclusion of their supper Wincanton had the innkeeper whistle up a chair to take her home. Major Wincanton morosely watched her off, then pulled up the collar of his cloak against the fine mist that was falling and began to make his way toward Russell Street.

He was comfortably ensconced in a wing chair in Amabel's withdrawing room, his feet propped on the fender of the fireplace, where he himself had set the logs ablaze, when he heard the sound of footsteps on the walkway and then a low murmur of voices just outside. He smiled mockingly when the front door opened and closed almost immediately. At least Lord Desmond had not been treated to the lingering, passionate farewell that had marked his last parting with Miss Fawnhope.

Swift footsteps and a rustle of satin crossed the hallway.

"Oh, Nellie—" Amabel halted abruptly on the threshold. "How the devil did you get in here, sir?"

He didn't bother to rise but gazed at her sardonically. "I bribed—*Nellie*, did you say?—that's how. Oh, she didn't come cheap, mind you. Cost me a bundle, in fact, to get her to unlock the door. Seems she was in a big hurry to get to the tavern. Funny thing, you know, she mentioned that she goes there practically every night. Like a mother to you, I believe you said? Or was it a watchdog? Anyhow, I did get the distinct impression that she was the reason you always—oh-so-reluctantly, of course—denied me entrance."

If he'd expected Miss Fawnhope to look disconcerted, he was doomed to disappointment. She merely shrugged. "What's a poor actress to do? I can't entertain male guests unchaperoned. And as you've just found out, Nellie flatly refuses to play that role. But since I don't wish to hurt anyone's feelings, I pretend otherwise. And"—her smile was meant to be disarming—"it's only a harmless little taradiddle, after all."

There was no answering grin from Major Wincanton. He continued to study her thoughtfully. "Yes, I'm sure you're capable of much better lies than that."

She flushed a bit but otherwise kept her composure. "I'll not rise to bait, Gareth, if you've come to quarrel. And now I must insist you leave. I'm sorry if you paid dearly to gain admittance, but indeed you should not have done so. You knew my stand on that. And besides, I'm very tired. I have a performance tomorrow and need my sleep."

"Oh, I won't take up a great deal of your time, Amabel." He indolently crossed one white-silk-clad ankle over the other. "But I did feel the need of privacy for our conversation. You see, I've come to tell you that you've won."

"I've won?" She walked into the room, tossing her Norwich silk shawl across a sofa back, and came to sit in an armchair opposite him. All her considerable thespian ability could not quite dampen the triumph in her eyes, though she spoke carelessly. "You should know that I haven't the slightest notion of what you're talking about. What have I won?"

"Me, of course. Let's speak plainly, Amabel. I'm tired of fencing. You'll not deny that the object of the game you've been playing was to bring me to heel?"

"I've played no game that I'm aware of."

"Oh, have you not indeed? Our courtship—if one could call it that—has been a veritable game of chess. Advance. Retreat. Attack. Followed by another strategic withdrawal. Then when the poor widgeon pursues, entrap him."

Her eyes narrowed. "You, sir, are being deliberately insulting."

"On the contrary. I'm being deliberately complimentary. Really, Miss Fawnhope, you should write a book on how to ensnare a reluctant gentleman. It would become a hornbook for the female sex and make your fortune."

"You're foxed, aren't you? I should have known." She rose to her feet. "Forcing yourself in here this way, spouting nonsense. I should have realized at once that you're disguised. But you do hold your drink like a gentleman, Major Wincanton. Could you not also behave like one and leave now?"

"Oh, do sit down, Bella."

"Don't call me Bella. You've picked that up from Nicky. I keep telling him I hate it."

"Then sit down, *Amabel*, my darling. Please. I promise you I'm not foxed in the slightest. And I beg pardon if I appeared insulting. I can only repeat that it was not my intention. Believe me, I am all admiration. You've done what I was determined you should not do. You've beaten me, Amabel. Thoroughly. Completely. I'm here merely to surrender."

She leaned forward in her chair; her eyes were shining. "Oh, Gareth. Do you really, truly mean it?"

"Oh, indeed I do. Really. Truly."

"Oh, darling, darling Gareth! You've made me deliriously happy!" Amabel cried as she jumped up and threw herself into his arms.

The interlude was brief but stormy, with much of the passion Wincanton had held in check now unleashed and Amabel responding with an enthusiasm that fueled his desire. It was only when he rose with her in his arms that she pulled her lips away. "Oh, no, Gareth," she managed to breathe huskily. "No, dearest. Not in there."

"Damnation, woman." He paused on the threshold of the dining room. "Where the devil is your bedchamber, for God's sake?"

But she was busy wriggling free of him, then standing on her own two feet. "Just never you mind about the bedchamber, Major Wincanton," she scolded him playfully. "After all we've been through together, I insist on doing the thing properly. The bedchamber can wait. We've the rest of our lives for that."

"Easy for you to say," he said, glaring. He personally might well expire at any moment from thwarted lust. But then he shrugged with resignation. "Oh, the hell with it. I've waited this long. A little longer won't kill me. Perhaps."

He let her lead him by the hand back to the sofa. There she untied his cravat, which had been crushed past all recognition of the Mathematical tie his valet had taken such pride in hours before, and fetched a cross-framed stool and placed it underneath his low-cut evening shoes. "I'll make us tea"—she smiled down at him tenderly—"and then we'll talk about our future."

God, but she was a coldhearted little baggage!

But later, after a half cup of the steaming, restorative brew, Amabel sensed that he was feeling much more the thing. She snuggled closer beside him, tucking her feet underneath her and letting her head rest against his shoulder. "First, where shall we live?" she muttered.

"Why, I collect I'll buy a house around here somewhere," he answered vaguely.

"Around here!" She stared up at him in surprise.

"Well, yes. Won't that suit?" His surprise matched hers.

"I'm amazed that you'd choose this particular neighborhood, that's all."

"Actually, I hadn't given that part a great deal of thought. I just supposed it was something you'd decide. Where would you prefer to live, then?"

"Grovesnor Square" was the prompt reply.

"Grovesnor Square!" Her answer jolted him. He almost blurted that he didn't like the notion above half. Still, he supposed it was not unthinkable. "But wouldn't that be a bit inconvenient for the theater?"

"Well, it's never stopped the carriage trade that I've ever noticed, so why I should not be able—" She broke off suddenly. "Surely you don't think I'll keep on working!"

Once again, he'd not thought that far. "Well"—he proceeded delicately—"I had just supposed you'd wish it. You've always seemed so dedicated to what you do. So ambitious. You talked of becoming another Mrs. Siddons, as I recall."

"And you wouldn't *mind*?"

"Why, no. At least I don't think so. Oh, I'll admit that I've always been a little jealous of your love scenes. And of the way the men in the audience ogle you. But at the same time I'll admit I've been proud, too. But you certainly don't need to perform if you don't wish it," he hastened to add as she continued to stare in disbelief. "You certainly will not need to. I plan to settle two thousand pounds a year on you, Amabel."

"Two thousand pounds!" she gasped. "Two thousand pounds!"

At first he thought she was simply overcome by his generosity. Slowly he realized she was incensed. "Come now," he protested. "I call the sum handsome. It's certainly far more than you're earning now. More, I suspect, than you ever will earn—at least for any length of time. You do realize I'm talking about a settlement for life, don't you? And as I was saying, you'll not have to continue on the stage, but if you choose to, well, then the peak of your earnings could put you fairly near the nabob class. But that part's up to you. For in either case you should be able to live comfortably—luxuriously, you might say. And any, er, *issue* should be well provided for."

"Issue?"

"Offspring. Oh, well then, dammit, *children*." He looked a bit embarrassed. "It's almost bound to happen. So I took that into consideration in arriving at a figure."

She was now sitting bolt upright and had distanced herself far enough to be able to look him directly in the eye.

"Now, let me get this all quite straight, Major Wincanton," she said with silky sweetness. "You are offering me a house—wherever—and two thousand pounds a year for life?"

"That's right."

"A carte blanche, in other words."

"You may call it that if you desire."

"A carte blanche!" Her voice rose in volume, quivered in anger. "And that's what this interview has been about? All your talk of surrender—capitulation—and you were thinking of a carte blanche? And just what did you think you were surrendering, Major Wincanton?"

"My freedom, dammit! God knows this kind of domestic arrangement was the last thing on earth I ever expected to enter into. But I've come to see I owe it to you, Amabel. Anything less than a commitment on my part would be unthinkable."

"Anything less than making me your mistress?"

"Anything less than putting our relationship on a permanent basis and seeing that you don't come to harm from it."

"You are all heart, Major Wincanton," she said between clenched teeth as she reached for the china teapot. The instinct that had saved him in many a hand-to-hand engagement did not fail him now. He dodged the missile and was on his feet when the pride of Josiah Wedgwood shattered on the wall.

"What the devil's come over you, Amabel?" he shouted. She reached for another projectile, and he began backing toward the door. "I'd thought to make you happy, and you've gone berserk." He sidestepped the flying cup, which then smashed into the paneling behind him. "God, but you're impossible—melting in my arms one minute, a termagant the next. Two thousand's more than handsome, Amabel. No use thinking you can do better—from me or from anyone—especially from that moon calf Keating. My God, woman, be reasonable. What did you expect?"

He thought it prudent to step through the door and slam it. A heartbeat later he heard the remaining cup and saucer explode on the other side. Nor was the heavy oak nearly thick enough to drown out her sobs.

"Expect? What did I expect? I expected you to marry me, you louse!"

Chapter Nine

*N*icholas Forbes *was still in bed, reluctant to get up.* It wasn't the luxury of that magnificent canopied and domed piece of furniture that seduced him, though he did realize he was growing far too fond of a mode of living almost as far out of his reach as a chance to become king. But it was the desire to think that kept him lying there.

And his thoughts turned to his ''little sister,'' though he sniffed aloud at the inappropriate term. Lovely little Amabel, with her air of fragility and her will of iron. Even when she was a child her ability to get her own way had been the stuff of legend. He grinned at the memory of the small face grown red with screaming and of the tiny, stamping feet. He'd paddled her little bottom once or twice himself, as he recalled—an occupation not without a certain appeal even now. He let that thought die aborning.

Amabel's methods for getting her own way had changed considerably, of course. But her determination to achieve that end was not one whit abated. He was sure of that. And he wondered how she was progressing in her plan to trap Wincanton into marriage. Nicky was certain—almost—that she'd met her match there. True, a cove should never predict how any man might behave around any woman. The laws of probability never seemed to apply to a confrontation of the sexes. But he was too well acquainted, partly through observation, more by reputation, with Wincanton's legendary coolness under fire to think that he would ever lose his head enough to form the sort of misalliance that Bella had in mind. Still, if anyone could bring it about, she could. That conclusion brought no joy. Nicky cursed himself for his dog-in-the-manger attitude. He should be wishing little Amabel success, instead of secretly hoping Wincanton would suddenly decide to renounce the world and enter a monastery. Small hope of that. With all his aristocratic ways, the major was a lusty one, no mistake.

Nicky's thoughts continued to dwell sourly upon Wincanton, and he took some small satisfaction in discovering that demigod's feet of clay.

For instance, he'd certainly been wrong about his Aunt Louisa. The idea of portraying her ladyship as a doddering old lady with failing senses—hardly able to see or hear, much less know what's what! If Wincanton could have seen his "ancient" aunt the way Nicky had when he'd blundered into the gold saloon, unaware that anyone was in there! Her clothes had been all every which way, and her cap had been lying on the floor behind the sofa arm as she and Sir George scrambled, red-faced, to their feet.

He grinned to himself at the recollection. So much for the antique old crone he'd been sent to gull. Still, to be fair about it, Wincanton hadn't seen her ladyship since his school days, and to a lad of that age, anyone over thirty was tottering hopelessly on the brink.

Nicky took a few moments to wonder just how well the major and his aunt might have dealt with each other if Wincanton had come to Bath himself. Not half so well as he and she had done, he'd bet a monkey. He took no small satisfaction in scoring off the aristocrat in at least one area.

For he and Lady Stoke had become the best of friends. There was nothing high in the instep about Louisa. Of course, she was actually no blood kin to the major, which probably accounted for it. She was, in fact, a kindly, lusty, fun-loving woman. And lady or no, she put him very much in mind of his own mother.

As he and Lady Stoke had left the outskirts of Bath recently, with him driving the curricle and the tiger riding behind, and were tooling down the road toward Weston village, her ladyship had come directly to the point. "I wished to get you alone to discuss Venetia."

Nicky had grown justifiably proud of the way he was learning to ape the manners of the gentry—a quick study, by Jove, if he did say so. But there was one area in which he had failed and could never hope to master, the ability of the aristocrat to make a nonperson of anyone in the servant class. Clearly the tiger's presence had not inhibited Louisa's conversation. Nicky, though, had been aware of the little thatch gallows's ears flapping all the while.

"I must say, my dearest Win," Louisa had continued, affectionately laying a gloved hand on his sleeve, "it's a delight to behold the change that's come over my niece since you arrived. No more silly talk about wearing caps and having nothing more to do with the other sex. I vow she's a different person altogether. And the transformation can be laid at your door entirely."

"Oh, I'm sure it would have happened anyhow," he'd answered modestly. "Time has a way of—"

"Oh, no," she'd interrupted him. "You do yourself an injustice if you believe that. Surely you must realize what an attractive young man you are, Wincanton. What lady could resist you for long?"

Nicky had heard a sudden snort behind them and had been hard put not to turn and give Jocko a set-down glare.

"Yes, it's easy enough to see the effect you've had on dear Venetia. What I wish to discover is the effect she's had on you." Her ladyship had then paused expectantly.

Nicky had thought it best to proceed cautiously. "I don't think I quite understand."

"Of course you do, Win dear. And I also understand you perfectly. You're thinking I'm meddling where I've no business to. But where Venetia's concerned, you see, I now stand *in loco parentis*."

"I beg your pardon?"

"Goodness, Win. Didn't they teach you any Latin in that expensive school of yours?"

"Er, yes, of course. At least they tried. But I fear mine's gone a trifle rusty. The Frenchies rarely shouted any Latin as they charged."

She'd chuckled. "Well, to put the whole thing in plain English, then, what with Venetia's father being a world away, I feel obliged to take his place and sound you out about her."

Nicky had begun to feel a constriction around his throat that had nothing to do with his carefully tied cravat. "Well, actually," he'd managed to say, "I really haven't thought that much on it."

"I know you haven't, m'dear," Lady Stoke had replied

97

patiently. "That's the object of this little talk. To get you to do just that. You like Venetia, don't you?"

"Yes, certainly." He'd had no problem there with sincerity.

"Well, then, that's all that's required, actually. What I wish to suggest—and, mind you, I'm not trying to push you into anything against your will—I simply wish you to consider making an offer for Venetia. Oh, I don't mean right away. I realize you need time to get accustomed to the notion. But I've grown more and more convinced that the two of you would deal quite well together. You enjoy each other's company. Your backgrounds are perfect for each other. You're both attractive—and of an age. And you're both excellent catches. I think it's a very good thing when neither party has to feel too obligated to the other in a marriage, don't you, Win? I don't know if you're acquainted with the size of Venetia's fortune, but—" And here Lady Stoke had gone on to mention a sum that had caused Nicky to suck in his breath and the tiger behind them to murmur, "Cor!"

"So you do understand, Win dear, just why I think you should seriously consider offering for Venetia. I know it would please your parents no end. And Venetia's father would be in raptures over such a match. Now, I don't wish to seem to pressure you. For there's no hurry about the thing. None at all. I only wished to put this tiny flea in your ear. For I'm convinced that a word to the wise is sufficient. Oh, I say—did that odd American who shocked himself with his silly kite say that, too?"

"Oh, God." Nicky now groaned aloud at the memory of that interview. "What a coil!" He roused himself to tug at the bellpull beside his bed. The chambermaid looked a bit surprised when he asked for tea to be brought in. He'd heretofore preferred to dress and go down to the

98

breakfast parlor. But he did not feel up to confronting Venetia quite yet. He only hoped that Lady Stoke had not put a flea in her ear as well.

He took advantage of his privacy to blow on his scalding tea while trying to recall every syllable of Lady Stoke's unsettling conversation. And for a bit he allowed himself to dream of being married to all that money. But he soon put a period to that fantasy. On stage the plot might unmask him as a pretender and then allow Lady Venetia to declare her undying love despite his humble origins, but in real life such a story line would never play. Oh, gentlemen did occasionally lose their heads and marry actresses. Amabel wasn't completely daft for pinning her hopes on the remote possibility. But a lady, marry a common actor? If such a thing had ever happened, he'd not yet heard of it.

So what the devil was he to do? Nothing.

After wrestling with the problem to the bottom of his teacup, he finally concluded that his best course of action was none at all. Lady Stoke had promised not to rush him. He had only a fortnight of impersonation left to go. Surely he could spend that length of time in Lansdown Crescent without being forced into any sort of declaration. After all, he'd been avoiding matrimonial traps for years. The only difference here was a matter of degree.

True to his latest resolution, Nicky managed to avoid being alone with Lady Venetia all that day. And when evening came, he pleaded the difficulty of standing around on his ''game leg'' as an excuse for not attending a private ball with their ladyships and Sir George Carstairs. The threesome was waiting for him in the hall, cloaked and expectant, when he limped heavily down the stairs and begged off apologetically.

"Oh, I say, Louisa," Porge broke into the ladies' sympathetic release of the suffering major, "do the rest of us have to go? Nothing but a boring crush, all Frederica's parties. We've got the perfect excuse, ain't we? Bad form to go off and leave an ailing guest.''

"Oh, I quite agree," Venetia seconded him. And so it was decided they'd all stay home with the invalid and provide their own entertainment.

In deference to the wounded hero's sensibilities, the evening began in a most sedentary manner. Venetia went to the pianoforte and began to play a soft and mournful air, while Lady Stoke pulled her tambouring hoop and a variety of colored silks out of the work table. Sir George was soon nodding in his chair and Nicky had smothered several prodigious yawns when Louisa protested, "For heaven's sake, Venetia, Win only has a hurt leg. He ain't dying. Don't you know anything but dirges? Or, better yet, why not come read to us?" She indicated the volume *Mysterious Warnings*, which still lay on the table, untouched since Nicky had examined it upon his arrival.

"Here, allow me." He roused himself and reached for the novel, feeling a need to exert himself before he drifted off with Sir George, who was now snoring rhythmically.

"Come over here by the light." Lady Stoke indicated the chair on the other side of the Egyptian-style candelabrum. "That is, if you're certain you feel up to it."

Nicky did. And the remarkable variance of his tone as he assumed the voices of different characters, plus the sepulchral way in which he read the creepy parts, soon had even Sir George wide-eyed and the ladies quaking in their chairs.

"Oh, do stop it!" Lady Louisa clapped her hands over her ears as Nicky emitted a low, prolonged, and ghostly moan. "I vow I'll not sleep a wink tonight as it is." She shivered pleasurably. "You've quite frightened me out of my wits, Win dear. I've never known anyone to read better, have you, Venetia? He actually brought the book to life. Why, I could see it all as if it were taking place before my very eyes.'' Again she shivered. ''We must do something else to get my mind off it, or else I'll be awake with the candle lit all night. Oh, I know! Charades! That is, if you don't think the exertion will be too much for your poor limb, Win dear. It might be best if you confine yourself to the guessing part and don't do any of the acting out. We'll excuse you this time, won't we?''

Though the other two agreed, it was not in Nicky's nature to be so retiring. He was soon caught up in the spirit of the game and insisted on taking his turn, during which he amazed them with the virtuosity of his performance. His enactment of the Seven Deadly Sins—without the aid of any makeshift stage props or costumes—earned him the spontaneous applause and vocal accolades of his tiny audience. Unaccustomed as he was to such an enthusiastic appreciation of his performances, Nicky was basking in the moment with professional pride when his euphoric mood was rudely shattered.

''I vow, Win,'' Lady Stoke gushed, ''for an instant I thought I must be in my box at the Theatre Royal. Why, if you'd been born a Cit, think of the career you might have had upon the stage!'' She gurgled at her own absurdity.

''Yes, it's wonderful that a military officer would be possessed of such a talent.'' Lady Venetia was looking at Nicky rather oddly, or so he imagined. ''Certainly your reading was the most moving that I've heard. And now your pantomime casts the rest of us entirely in the shade. You never cease to amaze me, Major Wincanton.''

Nicky managed to mumble some modest disclaimer, followed by an admission of having participated in his school theatricals. And then, when it was again his turn to do a charade, he lowered the level of his performance

101

to such a degree that his audience finally had to admit they hadn't had the slightest inkling he was trying to do the Labors of Hercules.

"Could've sworn you were that Hannibal cove crossing the Alps with a group of clumsy elephants," Sir George grumbled as he helped himself from the laden tea board that a footman had just placed before him.

And so the day ended for Nicholas Forbes as it had begun, with him lying in bed, reviewing his situation. You came close to blowing the gab, you curst loose screw! he berated himself as he tossed and turned. No telling what seeds of suspicion you may have planted.

He found consolation in another thought, however, as he blew out the candle and prepared for sleep. Of course, you did cover yourself quite well. The bit about school theatricals had shown quick thinking, and that god-awful turn at charades had made them forget all about his earlier, brilliant pantomime. Besides, why shouldn't a soldier like Wincanton have some acting talent? Look at that strutting peacock Napoleon. Now, there was a man who could have made it on the stage!

His mind, having been set at ease, now reverted to his drawing-room performance. By Jove, I was good tonight, wasn't I? he congratulated himself. No Edmund Kean, of course. Yet. But damned good, if I do say so.

Nicky basked for a moment longer in the memory of the others' admiration, then sighed heavily. Two more weeks to go. He turned on his stomach and buried his head beneath his pillow, ostrich-style. Well, a clever chap like him should be able to brazen it out for another fortnight without winding up arsy-varsy. Just as long as he kept out of the way of old acquaintants and didn't give in to another hen-witted acting urge.

Chapter
Ten

*Major Gareth Wincanton had just achieved his objec-
tive—seeing Miss Amabel Fawnhope alone—by the*
simple expedient of grabbing Lord Desmond Keating by
the collar and throwing him out of the actress's dressing
room. It was not an auspicious beginning for their interview.

Miss Fawnhope was seated at her dressing table, re-
moving the heavy stage makeup that she wore. The gaze
she fixed upon the major in the glass was steely. "You had
no right to do that," she said.

"How else was I to get a word with you? Don't worry—
the moon calf won't go away. Yet." He gave weight to the
final syllable.

"And what is that supposed to mean?"

"Simply that you've a head full of maggots if you expect Keating to marry you. Oh, I don't doubt he's willing enough." He staved off the retort forming on her lips. "Oh, asked you already, has he? Well, then you'd better get him to Gretna Green in a towering hurry, for someone's bound to have informed his papa, who should arrive any moment with the horsewhip to fetch his heir back home."

She wheeled angrily to face him. "You did that? How odious! How utterly despicable!"

"Climb off your high ropes, Amabel. You know I did no such thing. I hope I'm too much the gentleman to throw that kind of rub in your way. But I'll never know, for believe me, I wasn't even tempted. That sort of news doesn't need my help to travel fast. Some scandalmonger is probably banging his old lordship's ears right now. No, Amabel, *ma belle*, I fear you're backing another wrong 'un. If you're absolutely dead set on marriage, you'd best focus your chances on some Cit who's made a huge fortune in trade."

"Thank you for your advice, Major Wincanton," she replied with icy hauteur. "Now, having delivered yourself of it, will you kindly leave my dressing room?"

"Not till I've finished what I came to say."

"Then pray, be quick about it. I have a supper engagement, and if I can believe you, my escort may be snatched away before we come to the first remove. So don't detain me."

He lounged back against her doorway, which he'd locked, and ignored the fact that Lord Desmond's ear was undoubtedly pressed against it. "Am I to take it, then, that your attitude hasn't changed? I'd hoped that after you'd had a chance to cool down a bit, you'd see reason, Amabel."

"Reason?" Her voice rose an octave. "You think it *reasonable* to be your mistress?"

"Damn reasonable. You'd be established. And I can't—won't—marry you. I'd very much like to share your life, however."

"You'd like to go to bed with me, you mean. Come now, Major, let's not shy away from truth at this stage of the game."

"Very well, then, I'd like to go to bed with you. I've never denied that's mostly what this is all about. But you've other attractions as well. God knows you aren't exactly dull to be around." His smile was wry. "And perhaps if I were the country-gentleman type I'd snap my fingers at convention and we'd go rusticate together on one of my estates. But I've learned a few things about myself, you see. I found that I wasn't content to be a peacetime soldier, and I know I'll not be content to be a Bond Street beau for long. I need a challenge. Some kind of conflict. So I've decided on a political life, Amabel. And, to make no bones about it, a marriage to you would put a period to that particular ambition."

"Whereas keeping a mistress would speed your career right along!"

He shrugged away her indignation. "It wouldn't harm it. That's unjust, I know. But this is an unjust world. Think about it. You know my offer, Amabel."

"Indeed I do!" she blazed. "And I daresay you wouldn't be making it if my brother were still in town! I've half a mind to send for him. He'd give you what-for! Gentleman or no. Nicky would take a horsewhip to you, sir!"

"Nicholas is well aware of my intentions. And approves of them, let me add."

"That's a bald-faced lie!" Her hand closed on a rouge pot. "Nicky wouldn't hear of me being anybody's mistress!"

"Don't be goosish." He eyed her warily. "Any man of the world would be quick to see the advantages for you. But never mind now about Forbes. He has nothing to say in the matter. It's your decision." Wincanton was unlocking the door as he spoke. "I'm through playing games, Amabel. I'm here for your final answer."

He got it. She flung the pot at him just as he'd jerked the door wide open. It struck Lord Desmond in the chest, where its contents played havoc with the black superfine of that dandy's long-tailed evening coat and detracted from the intricate folds of his pristine starcher.

It had been Lady Venetia Lowther's idea that "Major Wincanton" must see Prior Park, Nicholas Forbes's that the treat should be shared by Lady Stoke and Sir George Carstairs, and Lady Stoke's that the young couple should be left to their own devices.

The shared carriage ride to the stately home, built in the mid-1700s by Ralph Allen, a former postmaster and social leader of Bath and owner of the Bathstone quarries, rather frustrated Lady Stoke's scheme for the afternoon but suited Nicky to a tee. It was his notion to avoid all possible pitfalls for the remainder of his stay. This included keeping clear of the city and of the danger of running into old acquaintances, either his or the major's, there and nipping in the bud any opportunity that might lead to a romantic entanglement between himself and Lady Venetia.

He had, however, underestimated the strong-willed determination of Lady Stoke. Upon arriving at the park, the foursome left their carriage as a unit. They stood together upon the mansion's terrace, gazing at the panorama it overlooked. Mr. Allen, under the influence of Alexander Pope, so it was said, had planted trees on either side of a valley that sloped downward from the mansion, so that the eye was automatically focused, as though peering through a giant spyglass, upon the distant white-stoned lovely city of Bath.

After admiring this breathtaking view for a few awed moments and speculating upon the possibility of rain, the party set out—still together. Their walk wandered through the trees that lined one side of the grassy expanse where cattle grazed. It would eventually lead them to the Paladian Bridge, one of the chief wonders to be seen at Prior Park.

But they had not traversed three-quarters of that distance when Lady Stoke, spying a convenient rustic bench, turned an ankle and declared herself unable to walk another step.

Nicky was all for making an "armchair" with Sir George's help and carrying her back to the carriage. But her ladyship would have none of it. Not for anything would she spoil the opportunity for her guest to explore the grounds. Dear Porge, who like her had been there countless times before, would keep her company. But Venetia must act as dear Win's guide. And on no account must her trifling injury be allowed to ruin their outing. As long as she kept her weight off her tiresome ankle, she could assure them, it pained her not at all.

Nicky had no choice. He set out alone with Lady Venetia. But when he realized that all her interest was fixed upon the marvels of the park, which she delighted in previewing for him, he soon relaxed and began to enjoy their sightseeing. One treat they must not miss, it seemed, was a spot known popularly as Pope's Grotto, copied from one in the poet's Twickenham estate. What's more, the very dog that the great man had presented to Mr. Allen was buried there, with a touching inscription, "Weep not," engraved on a flagstone by Pope himself. It was Nicky's opinion that, poet or not, he personally could have come up with something a great deal better, but in light of his guide's enthusiasm, he decided to keep that sentiment to himself.

Just as Venetia and Nicky left the shelter of the trees, the low-lying clouds that had almost dissuaded them from making this excursion decided to open up and do their worst. "Oh, my goodness!" she exclaimed, and with an alacrity that both astonished and impressed her companion, she ran for the Paladian Bridge.

The rain was coming down in sheets now, wind-driven, and when Venetia reached the covered structure, the sole of her half boot slipped on the wet stone floor. This could have caused a very nasty fall indeed, had not Nicky been right there to catch her. As it was, the results of this timely intervention were even more disastrous.

For upon finding the delectable Lady Venetia encircled in his arms with her face uplifted toward his in gratitude, Nicky completely lost his head and kissed her. The kiss, despite the water streaming from her bonnet and the curly brim of his beaver hat, turned out to be such an agreeable occupation that the thought of terminating it never even occurred to him.

And after the initial shock of being so accosted had quickly fled, to be replaced by other, far more interesting sensations, Venetia had no impulse, either, to put a period to this enlightening experience. For it had come to her as a complete surprise to learn that she had never actually been kissed before. Oh, she had thought that she had been. And had considered the activity decidedly overrated. Now she knew that the cool and calculated busses Mr. Fletcher Langford had planted upon her cheek and, rarely, upon her lips could not even qualify as imitation kisses. Major Gareth Wincanton, however, was assuredly delivering the real thing.

There was no way of knowing just how long this pleasurable state of affairs might have continued, had it not been interrupted by the unexpected arrival of Sir George and Lady Stoke.

The downpour had wrought a miraculous cure. Her ladyship had discovered not only that she could support her weight on the injured ankle but that she could outdistance Sir George to the shelter of the Paladian structure and arrive a step before him while Nicky and Venetia's lovemaking was still at a fever pitch.

"Oh, my goodness, Porge!" her ladyship called to her winded companion while clapping her hands with delight. "Would you look at this! Well, what have you to say now, sir? Did I not predict that we'd soon be wishing these two lovebirds happy?"

The two lovebirds sprang apart—Venetia, embarrassed; Nicky, appalled.

"Yes, indeed you did, Louisa. Congratulations, m'boy." Sir George, deeply moved, clapped Nicky on the shoulder. "Couldn't be more pleased, b'gad, if you were me own son."

"Oh, I say!" Nicky tried to protest but choked.

Venetia, recovering more quickly, filled the breach. "Oh, really, Aunt Louisa, you mustn't jump to such conclusions. You much mistake the matter, I assure you. Win has not offered for me."

"Only because we blundered in and interrupted" was

the arch reply. "Pray, don't mind us, Win dear. Go right ahead."

"I say now, really! That's hardly—"

"Necessary?" Sir George chuckled. "I should think not myself. Not after the way you two were going at it. Fair put us to the blush, didn't it, old girl?"

"Yes, and I shudder to think, Venetia, what your dry stick of a father would have to say. Well, the sooner I send a notice to the *Gazette*, the better it will be for all concerned."

There was a long and pregnant pause. Lady Venetia was the one who finally broke it. "If it's what Win wishes," she said, feeling her way tentatively.

"Well, we all know what Win wishes." Lady Stoke's laugh was bawdy. "La, if we hadn't come along just when we did, I vow he'd have had you on the floor, like as not."

"Aunt Louisa!"

"No use coming all over missish at this late date, Venetia. You were enjoying every minute of it."

Nicky felt himself being swept away like the rain-swollen waters that were gathering momentum underneath the bridge they were standing on. He made a last, valiant attempt to save the situation. "Oh, but you mustn't notify the paper just yet, Louisa. I mean to say it wouldn't be the thing. I'll need to write Venetia's father for permission."

"Nonsense! All the way to Brazil and back? Why, that would take you donkey's years. And it ain't as though Venetia's not of age. The sooner the better, that's what I say. Don't you agree, m'dear?"

She turned toward her niece, who hesitated just a fraction longer before murmuring agreement.

"Well, then, that's all settled." Lady Stoke beamed with satisfaction. "Do you suppose Cook included some champagne in the picnic basket? If not, we'll simply toast the happy couple with claret, Porge. Look—the rain's let up. Does anyone see a rainbow anywhere? There ought to be one to mark the occasion. Oh, well, never mind. One can't have everything. Do let's hurry back before the rain starts up again. I'm sure we've seen all we need to see of Prior Park.''

Her ladyship kept up a constant stream of congratulatory chatter all the way back to their carriage. She overflowed with plans and predictions for the young couple's future happiness.

Nicky, however, could not hear a single word of it above the persistent roaring in his ears.

Chapter
Eleven

*I*t was fortunate that Amabel Fawnhope had nothing at hand to throw but the copy of the *Gazette* she was reading when she saw the notice of Lady Venetia Lowther's engagement to Major Gareth Wincanton. She hurled it viciously, but, in the manner of paper, it merely flapped its way across her counterpane to land on the floor at the foot of her four-poster. She immediately retrieved it to read the notice once again. Having satisfied herself that no hallucination was involved, Miss Fawnhope let loose a flood of tears, more in rage than in sorrow, then spent most of the afternoon lying in bed with a wet cloth over her eyes, trying to repair the damage from such self-indulgence.

The treatment did not work as well as she might have wished, which proved a very good thing, for her red-rimmed eyes gave credence to her story of the death of a dear, dear friend when she asked for leave to attend the funeral.

Major Wincanton learned secondhand the news of his betrothal. He was drinking a thoughtful second cup of tea, after having polished off a breakfast of ham and eggs, when Lord Piggot-Jones and Mr. Bertram "Sprig" St. Leger ran the disapproving gauntlet of his butler and his valet to interrupt his reverie.

Two minds with but a single thought, they had converged on the doorstep of Number Four, St. James's Square, each clutching his copy of the *Gazette*. Now they vied with each other to see who would be first to break the news.

In the end, since Wincanton's glare was hardly encouraging, they both simply thrust their copies toward the major, index fingers pointing to the cogent paragraph.

Major Wincanton prided himself on a superior intellect. But in this instance he was slower to comprehend than Miss Fawnhope had been. He was forced to give the item a third reading, with no time out for throwing, before he fully took it in.

His friends waited anxiously for an explosion that did not come, however. It belatedly occurred to both that their eagerness might be their undoing, should this turn into a classic case of "kill the messenger," so they backed off a discreet distance as he read. But whereas the soldier had first turned white, then fiery red, he otherwise managed to keep a tight rein on his emotions.

After a lengthy silence, the Sprig dared to break it. "By gad, he's won it!" he crowed unwisely.

Wincanton's furious eyes impaled him. "What the devil are you talking about?"

"The wager. He's pulled it off! He's won it! What an impersonation! I never dreamed he'd be able to carry the thing so far. And you actually said, Piggot-Jones, that Nicky couldn't play Little Jack Horner if you gave him a Christmas pie. Those were your very words!"

"He ain't won yet," the other said darkly. "What he's done, it appears, is overreach himself, the cocky devil. The time ain't up yet, by any means. And he'll never be able to keep up the impersonation now. Too complicated by half is my opinion. Oh, I say, Win, just who *is* Lady Venetia Lowther?"

"How the devil should I know?"

The vicious retort sent the visitors off into gales of laughter, despite the ever-present threat of a combat hero's temper put on the boil.

"Oh, lord," the Sprig managed to gasp as they subsided, "that's rich. He's no notion at all of the gel that he's betrothed to."

This sally set them off again. Then, when they'd partially recovered for a second time, Piggot-Jones managed to ask, "What are you going to do about it, Win?"

"Go to Bath."

"But you can't do that!" St. Leger protested, suddenly sobered. "The wager! Have you forgotten the wager? You'd be throwing a rub in Nicky's way. Ain't sporting to interfere in any way that might decide the outcome of a bet."

"Damn the bet!" Major Wincanton spoke through teeth that were tightly clenched.

An hour later, in a curricle hired from Tattersall's, he was speeding down the Bath Road at an alarming rate.

His two friends, driving Piggot-Jones's rig, followed at

a discreet distance, ostensibly to see that the terms of the wager were not violated, but covertly determined to miss none of the fun.

And at five o'clock the following morning, after having been assessed three halfpence per pound for five pounds of baggage over the limit, Miss Amabel Fawnhope boarded the public coach. She, too, was bound for Bath.

Chapter
Twelve

As Major Wincanton proceeded down Bath's Cheap Street in the late afternoon of the day following his arrival, he caught sight of a familiar vehicle. He skillfully weaved his way through the congestion of carriages, horsemen, carts, and crossing pedestrians and managed to pull abreast of his own curricle. It was necessary for him to shout "Jocko!" in an imperious voice to get the driver's full attention, which was firmly fixed on the barque of frailty he was striving to impress. The tiger looked around with some annoyance.

"Can't it wait, guv? I'm bloody busy. Oh, I say, where'd you get the rig? Oh, my God, it's you! Beg pardon, sir. I thought—"

"I know what you thought. I need to talk to you."

They pulled off the busy thoroughfare, and while the tiger's companion held the horses, he jumped down to secure the major's cattle. His employer joined him at the horses' heads. "You might begin by explaining what you're doing tooling that lightskirt around town in my curricle."

It was not an auspicious beginning to what could only be an awkward interview, but Jocko did his best. "Why, exercising the beasts, that's wot. You've no notion, guv—*sir*, I means to say—of 'ow that imposture neglects 'em. I knew as 'ow you'd want 'em kept fit, sir."

"And I suppose you also knew I'd want you to parade that baggage around Bath in my rig. But never mind that just now. What's been going on?"

"Well, I daresay as 'ow you must know the meat of the matter, else you wouldn't be 'ere." The tiger's attempt to suppress a grin was only partially successful.

"If you mean I've read the notice of my betrothal, then you're right. So enlighten me. Who the deuce is Lady Venetia Lowther?"

After the tiger had filled him in on the background and appearance of his fiancée, Wincanton asked drily, "Aside from his obvious romantic success, how has the actor gotten along? Would you say my aunt's at all suspicious?"

"Lor' no, sir." Despite all better judgment, Jocko gave the grin free rein. "Plays you to a treat, 'e does. Much as I 'ates to admit it, I must say I underestimated the fellow. Lady Stoke's fair eating from his 'and, and 'e's nailed down a fortune in Lady Venetia as I've 'eard tell would make King Midas jealous. You might go so far as to say 'e makes a more thorough job of being Major Wincanton than you do, sir."

"You might say it if the actor paid your wage. As he or someone else may soon need to do," Wincanton snapped.

"Now, I suggest you get rid of your doxy in short order and see to it my grays are properly rubbed down before they're stabled."

This time Jocko Hodges's "Yes, sir" was a model of subservience.

"And one more thing," the major called as he climbed aboard his hired curricle. "Don't tell the actor that you've seen me. I think it best if I throw him that particular cue."

The trouble with that notion was that for probably the first time in his life, Major Wincanton found himself at a loss as to how best to proceed. He'd come haring down to Bath, blood in his eye, but what the devil was he to do now that he was here?

His inclination was to drive straight up Lansdown Hill to the Crescent, expose the actor for the fraud he was, confess his part in the hoax, break the engagement, and take his medicine. That was what he'd like to do, but he knew he couldn't. And it was not the presence of Piggot-Jones and St. Leger who'd come to Bath to ensure that he do no such thing that stopped him. Wincanton knew the code without their prompting. He could not intervene in any way that might influence the outcome of the wager without earning the condemnation of his acquaintances. He'd have to watch his step very carefully. His honor as a gentleman was at stake.

When he emerged from the White Hart the next morning, Wincanton was still mulling over how best to proceed. He was depending upon a brisk walk to clear away some of the cobwebs resulting from a near-sleepless night and was mentally composing a note to Forbes, asking the actor to meet him in some out-of-the-way place, when his thoughts were interrupted by a female voice hailing him.

He had paused and turned before he was struck by the folly of responding to "Oh, Major Wincanton!" He now saw, hurrying his way, an attractive young lady who wore a cherry pelisse and was laden down with parcels. She was almost upon him when he saw her dark eyes widen in surprise, followed by a confusion that rapidly turned into embarrassment. "But you aren't! Oh, I do beg your pardon! I mistook you for my fiancé."

Venetia continued to look Wincanton up and down in some bewilderment while he appraised her just as closely. Well, at any rate he couldn't fault the actor's taste. She was a very personable young lady.

"I'm flattered by the mistake, ma'am." He recovered enough to reply in a manner worthy of Nicholas Forbes. "Your fiancé is a most fortunate man."

His obvious admiration was rather disconcerting to Venetia. "It's astonishing how much you do resemble him. Why, you even have the same slight limp. Oh, I beg your pardon." She was aghast at her tactlessness. He might be sensitive about his infirmity.

"Not at all. That really is a coincidence." A limp, for God's sake! Trust an actor to overdo.

"And then there's the same hair coloring. Win says that red-haired people—but of course!" The light had begun to dawn. "Why, you must be Mr. . . . Forbes, was it? I believe that was the name. Yes, I'm sure now of it. Are you by chance Mr. Nicholas Forbes?"

It was on the tip of the major's tongue to emphatically deny it. But instinct told him that a third look-alike in the farce his fellow club members had created would strain credulity a bit too much. "However did you know?" he inquired cautiously.

"Why, some friend of yours made the same mistake that I did—in reverse, of course. Oh, I say, are you by chance an actor?"

"No!" He realized he'd been a shade too vehement, but

he was damned if he was going to take on Forbes's identity. The name was bad enough. He smiled to correct the impression that he'd just been insulted. "Actually, I'm a soldier. Or was, I should say. That's why I thought you really were addressing me," he said, improvising. "I didn't quite catch the name but did hear you say 'major.' "

"This really is the oddest thing."

"Isn't it? I say, I noticed a tearoom back there, the way we came. Couldn't we have a cup of tea and discuss it further?"

Venetia's conscience began to form polite excuses, for what he had suggested was totally improper. On the other hand, she was formally engaged now. If, as Aunt Louisa claimed, a married lady could do whatever pleased her, well, surely an affianced one was allowed a little license. Besides, she convinced herself, she was simply parched with thirst.

The major ended her vacillation by the simple expedient of relieving her of her parcels and taking her elbow.

When they were settled in at a small table with a pot of Indian tea and a supply of the ubiquitous Bath buns, he said, "Tell me more about your fiancé. I must admit it's a strange feeling to learn I have a double."

"Actually, the resemblance is only slight, now that I've seen you better. But you are both of a height"—she delicately skirted around mentioning the limp again—"and most of all, there's your hair. Major Wincanton's is of the same brilliant shade."

"But then, of course, he's better-looking," Wincanton offered before he thought.

She appeared to think it over rather seriously. "No, I would not say so" was the verdict. Then, for some inexplicable reason, she blushed. "Were you on the Peninsula?" she asked to cover her confusion.

Not wishing to overdo the parallels between "Major Wincanton" and himself, he started to deny it. But the devil with coincidence, he decided. It was a large army, after all. "As a matter of fact, I was." He went on to elaborate.

Lady Venetia proved to be a marvelous listener. She had long been fascinated by Wellington's campaigns, but her curiosity had gone largely unsatisfied. Her fiancé, it seemed, had spoken little of his experiences, and she'd been reticent about quizzing him.

The major was rather surprised at this revelation. He would have expected Nicky Forbes to be expansive on that particular subject, since it was the one place that the actor's background meshed with that of the man he impersonated. Wincanton's conclusion was that the ex-private was afraid of revealing too much of the common soldier's point of view in any account he might give of the Peninsula Campaign.

The major was impressed with the intelligent questions his listener asked and with her keen interest in the political aspects of the Napoleonic defeat. It pleased him to learn that her father was a diplomat and that she'd spent several years in Spain. Their tea grew cold as they traded their impressions of that fascinating country. Later Wincanton realized that this was a first for him. He'd never had a serious conversation with a woman before, let alone given such credence to the judgment of a member of the other sex.

"Oh, my goodness, the time!" Venetia woke up to the fact that she'd spent the better part of an hour in the tea shop. "My aunt will wonder what's become of me. I'm to fetch a particular silk she needs for her tambouring. Oh, well"—she smiled—"Aunt Louisa is an indifferent needlewoman and may be just as glad to have had an excuse to stay idle." She rose from the table and thanked the major politely for the tea. "You must call soon." She found refuge in formality. "My fiancé is also staying with our aunt. I'm sure he'll wish to meet you. You have so much in common, you're certain to become friends."

That was a possibility he'd not bet on, no matter how foxed, he told himself as he escorted her ladyship outside. "Thank you. I shall be pleased to call," he lied, "if you'll give me your direction."

Here was just one more devilish complication, he realized as she gave him her address. He didn't dare come face-to-face with his Aunt Louisa. She was bound to grow suspicious if she ever saw Forbes and him together, and it wouldn't take her long to sort them out. The Sprig was right. He should never have left London. Still, when Venetia smiled up at him shyly and said good-bye, he found it difficult to regret his folly to the degree required.

As he walked slowly back to his hotel, Major Gareth Wincanton was feeling more confused and less in charge of circumstances than he ever had throughout the course of his entire life. He sought the sanctuary of his room, anxious to blow a cloud and spend some time in quiet thought. But this bit of escapism was denied him. He opened his door, to be greeted by the accusing faces of his friends.

Lord Piggot-Jones fired the first volley. "I must say I'm shocked."

Right behind him Mr. St. Leger brought up his guns. "Ain't the thing at all, Wincanton. Not gentlemanly. Unsportsmanlike."

"What the devil are you two ranting on about?"

"No use acting the innocent with us. We saw you in the tea shop. Chattering away like anything. And we know who the lady was."

"And so?"

"And so you are deliberately interfering with the out-come of our wager. That's low, Win, it really is." The Sprig was awash with righteous indignation. "A gentle-man would have stayed in London."

"A gentleman would not have entered into a betrothal as someone else."

"Yes, but then Nicky *ain't* a gentleman. We all knew that when we put up our blunt. Couldn't expect *him* to behave like one, now, could we? But yours is a different case entirely. And we're disappointed in you—there's the long and short of it. I could halfway understand your need to talk to Nicky and find out what's what. But to introduce yourself to your fiancée right off the bat, that really is the outside of enough. By the by," he came down off his high ropes long enough to ask, "how did she take it?"

"She didn't. That is to say, of course I didn't tell her who I am. And if you had come along a little earlier, you'd know I didn't seek her out. She spoke to me." He went on to explain what had happened.

"Thinks you're Nicky, eh?" Lord Piggot-Jones sud-denly peered at Wincanton through his quizzing glass as if to establish his true identity. "God, this is confusing."

"No, she doesn't. That is to say, she believes Nicholas Forbes is my name, but not all the rest of it— Oh, the devil. You know what I mean."

"Can't say I do, really," the Sprig said, sighing, "but I am relieved to hear you didn't blow the gab. Still and all, it certainly would've been a dashed sight better if you'd stayed in London with your little ladybird, where you be-longed."

Wincanton's eyes narrowed dangerously. "If by any chance, St. Leger, you are referring to Miss Fawnhope, pray, use her proper name."

"Beg pardon, I'm sure." The Sprig turned scarlet. The major nodded a curt acknowledgment of the apology and offered port. When the friends parted company a little later, an uneasy truce prevailed.

Nicholas Forbes, however, was not as fortunate in his mental state at the conclusion of an interview that took place at approximately the same time. Lady Venetia had returned from her shopping expedition and found him reading in the library.

"Oh, there you are, Gareth. I've been looking for you everywhere. The oddest thing just happened. You can't imagine whom I met on Milsom Street."

Chapter
Thirteen

The council of war that took place in the White Hart that afternoon was unsatisfactory to all parties concerned. After Lady Venetia's bombshell burst, Nicholas Forbes had come rushing down Lansdown Hill at the first opportunity. He'd been spotted entering the inn by Lord Piggot-Jones and Mr. St. Leger, who were lolling in the public parlor. They had insisted upon accompanying him to Major Wincanton's rooms in order to protect their interests.

The two red-haired men eyed each other with stony faces. It was the genuine Major Wincanton who was now grateful for the hours spent over cards that had schooled him to hide all emotion. For he was jarred by the change in Nicholas Forbes, a change that he'd have been hard put to define but that nonetheless was evident.

There had always been something entirely too flash about the actor, a showiness smacking of the stage. So of course the exquisitely understated gray coat and biscuit pantaloons he himself had provided made a difference. But this did not begin to account for all the change. It was as if in playing the gentleman, Nicholas had become one.

It occurred to Wincanton that Lady Venetia just might marry the actor anyhow, once he'd been exposed. Forbes was a good-looking devil; there was no denying that. Wincanton refused, however, to draw any parallel between his own infatuation with Amabel and Lady Venetia's possible feelings for the actor. No, by God, it had to be Major Wincanton, scion of one of England's oldest families and grandson of an earl, that Venetia had agreed to marry. What was it Jocko had said, though? "He makes a more thorough job of being Major Wincanton than you do." Well, it was time to put a period to this kind of thinking. Self-doubt could prove habit-forming. He'd had enough of it.

"How's Amabel?" Nicky asked abruptly as he commandeered the wing chair closest to the fireplace and let his two companions make do with an upholstered mahogany settee.

Wincanton, however, refused to be upstaged and remained upon his feet, lounging against the mantel. "Amabel's quite well," was his nonrevealing answer. He'd be damned if he'd advertise his failure in that department, too.

"Well, what's to be done?" The Sprig tried to cut through the small talk and stared expectantly at Wincanton.

The major could have told him the half-baked plan he'd

formed during his ride down from London. It had been simple enough. He'd meant to tell the actor to get out of Bath as soon as his month was up, leaving a note behind, confessing his impersonation. The note would explain that he'd been out of work and out of funds and had seized upon a known resemblance to Major Wincanton in order to worm his way into their household for free board and lodging. In no way would Wincanton have had to be connected with the deception. He could show up innocently upon his aunt's doorstep anytime he wished.

But that plan was worthless now. Today Venetia had met him as "Nicholas Forbes" and would know that he had been a party to the flimflam. She was bound to despise him for it. He found the thought of that too lowering to dwell on.

"I asked you, Wincanton, what's to be done?" the Sprig repeated.

"How should I know?" was the terse reply.

"Nicky?" The Sprig's expectant look was a tribute to the actor's resourcefulness. But Nicky's shrug was eloquent. The Sprig looked shocked, then sighed heavily and took charge himself.

"I think we should consider that the terms of the wager were violated by extenuating circumstances. What I mean to say is that when Win here came to Bath, as he'd no right to do, it put a spanner in the works. I thereby declare Nicholas Forbes the winner."

A howl of protest rose from Lord Piggot-Jones, who stood to lose a bundle. "Now, just you hold on, St. Leger. 'Extenuating circumstances' be damned! What I mean to say is, when you place a bet on something or other, you simply take it for granted there'll be extenuating circumstances. Why do you think they call it gambling? Because of all those extenuating circumstances, that's why. Your horse pulls a tendon. That's an extenuating circumstance. Your dog gets sick before he kills more rats than the other cove's mongrel. That's an extenuating circumstance. The bruiser you put your blunt on in the ring—''

''We get the picture, Piggot-Jones,'' Major Wincanton said, breaking in upon the tirade.

''The point I'm making''—the other stuck doggedly to his guns—''is that it ain't fair to call off the bet now. Nobody ever actually said you couldn't go to Bath if you took the notion. And you've just explained that you didn't blow the gab to Nicky's fiancée, which would really be too low for words. I say the wager stands.''

A fierce argument then broke out. The two men most involved took no part but eyed each other surreptitiously.

''I think we have to let Nicky off the hook,'' the Sprig insisted for the dozenth time.

''Why the devil should we? No one told him to offer for the girl. Talk about your extenuating circumstances! Now, there's a— My word, Nicky, you don't actually mean to marry her before your time's up, do you?''

Judging from their expressions, Nicky could see that the gentlemen present hadn't thought of such a horrifying possibility.

''Of course not. Don't be a gudgeon.'' The Sprig recovered first. ''He couldn't marry as Wincanton. Wouldn't be legal—not even to mention moral—don't you know.''

But the three were glaringly aware of the golden opportunity afforded the penniless actor. Such a marriage would be illegal, right enough. But it also would create a climate for blackmail, the high price of hushing a scandal.

''I'd never let you get away with it,'' Wincanton said between clenched teeth.

''Get away with what?'' Nicky asked innocently as he rose to his feet, drawing on the major's best pair of gray kid gloves. He was well aware of what was going on in he others' minds and was thoroughly enjoying their agitation. "I plan to carry out the terms of our wager as set down in Brooks' betting book. And if any of you *gentlemen*"—he sneered at the word—"interfere in those terms in any way, well, it will behoove me to report that breach of faith to whoever's in charge of that sort of thing. Surely the club has a review committee to see that everything's right and tight? If not, they can always form one."

That seemed a good-enough speech to exit on, so the actor did so, closing the door emphatically behind him.

On his way back up Lansdown Hill, Nicky chuckled to himself over Major Wincanton's discomfort. Let the stiffrumped toff stew in his own juice a bit. Do him good. Nicky took pleasure in dwelling on the major's out-of-joint proboscis; it gave him a reprieve from his own problems. But halfway to the Crescent he reluctantly began to review his own situation.

For it wasn't the bet alone that was holding him in Bath. And the others wronged him gravely when they thought he'd go through a marriage with blackmail in mind. He'd seen the opportunity right away, of course. He was no fool. Nor was he a blackguard. The truth, which he now acknowledged for the first time, was that he was being downright quixotic. Chivalrous. Or, better yet, a hopeless idiot. Nicky could hardly believe it of himself, but there it was. He simply couldn't bear the thought of being the second fiancé in a row to humiliate Lady Venetia Lowther. He was convinced she'd never recover from such a double blow to her self-esteem. He was buying time now to allow her to call off the engagement to "Major Wincanton" of her own volition. Not because she was once more forced by a shattering discovery to do so but simply because she would have decided that they wouldn't suit. Then later, if she should ever find out she'd been deceived, at least she would have the satisfaction of knowing that she'd sent the scoundrel packing. She might be angry, but she would not be hurt by the experience.

His instinct told him that Venetia was already regretting their betrothal as much as he was. For from the moment that Lady Stoke had sprung her trap, their relationship had changed. The free and easy friendship they'd developed had deteriorated into awkward politeness. And on the rare occasions when they were alone together, Venetia carefully avoided mentioning their engagement, a state of affairs that Nicky welcomed.

But it was not only the subject she avoided; he was convinced she was avoiding him as well, a second circumstance that he rejoiced in. The only time she had actually sought him out was after her meeting with Wincanton.

Nicky mulled that over as he walked along, still limping out of force of habit. She hadn't seemed at all suspicious of the coincidence. If he hadn't just become a reformed punter, he'd bet on that. Still, when she'd had more time to think about it— Damn Wincanton's eyes! The Sprig was right. He'd no business leaving London. Things were already at sixes and sevens without him coming on the scene to mess them up still more!

From the bow window of her bedchamber, Venetia watched him walking down the Crescent and caught her breath. "Oh, it's only Win, you pea goose." She corrected her misapprehension, at the same time acknowledging to herself that she'd actually been watching for Mr. Forbes to pay his visit. Her cheeks burned at that damning bit of insight. It was almost four o'clock, late now for morning calls. He wasn't going to come. And she didn't feel up to facing Wincanton at the moment. Perhaps exercise would help clear up some of the confusion she was feeling. She quickly put a rose gros de Naples spencer jacket over her pale pink round dress and chose her most becoming high-crowned bonnet to wear with it.

Venetia would have vowed that her direction was aimless, her route chosen from force of habit. When she did wake up to the fact that her feet had carried her to the heart of the city, it became necessary, for her peace of mind, to invent an acceptable reason for having done so. Hence she was hurrying to Smith's haberdashers when Gareth came driving down Stall Street and spied her.

"Lady Venetia!" he called, and she didn't really need to turn around to discover who it was. Even so, her heart skipped a beat in confirmation at the sight of the man in the five-caped greatcoat who was wearing his curly beaver centered on his head, not tilted rakishly, in the style favored by her fiancé.

"Could I take you wherever you're going?"

Since he was clogging the street's traffic with his curricle, it seemed the thing to do to hurry over and be handed up.

"Now where to?" He smiled down at her as he flicked his reins.

"To Smith's shop." She smiled back.

"You'll have to tell me where that is. I'm a stranger to Bath."

"Oh, my goodness, we've passed it!" She'd been just two doors away when he'd picked her up. He glanced back over his shoulder, saw the swinging sign, and laughed. She joined in, though she felt rather foolish.

"Surely your errand can wait, then. I was just going to explore a bit. And I need a guide. What would be a scenic drive?"

"Have you seen Sydney Gardens yet?" she asked, and, when he said no, pointed the way to Pulteney Street.

"You haven't told me, Major Forbes," she said as they crossed the shop-lined Florentine-style bridge, "just why you've come to Bath."

"For the same reason everyone comes, I collect."

"Surely not for a course of the waters. I'll not believe it."

"Why not? The Pump Room is certainly popular. The stuff must be good for something."

"For gout and rheumatism, perhaps, though I'm not convinced of it entirely. But no one your age comes to Bath for the waters. Indeed, according to Aunt Louisa, no one who is not at least an octogenarian comes here at all."

"No? Are you trying to tell me it won't cure my limp?" he teased her. "Well, I am dished. I'd set my heart on it. Still," he added casually, "you did say that your fiancé is similarly afflicted. And if it has not cured him—well, there's no use hoping. Oh, by the by, since you've pointed out that he and I resemble each other, I trust he's not an octogenarian."

"Hardly," she said, laughing. "Oh, I see what you mean. But he came to visit our Aunt Louisa."

"And met you? Fortunate fellow. Just goes to show, I expect, that it pays to be familial. I must make a note of that."

The look he gave her was so intense that she quickly launched into a catalogue of the treats that would have been in store for him in Sydney Gardens if only he'd chosen to come in the summertime. Why, on gala nights there were music, singing, transparences, fireworks, illuminations, all sorts of delights. Vauxhall in London could boast of little more, she assured him as he drove his rig through the pleasure garden entryway.

When she pointed out the labyrinth just beyond the carriage drive, he insisted upon stopping to explore it.

"At your own peril," she said with a laugh. "I've been in it once before and must warn you that I became hopelessly lost."

"Well, obviously you got out. How did you manage?"

"I'm ashamed to say that Aunt Louisa and I simply stood and shouted till our friend Sir George Carstairs came and rescued us. It pains me to say so, but men as a rule do seem better at directions than we women. I hope now for both our sakes that I don't generalize. Are you good at finding your way through mazes, Major Forbes?"

"I was used to think so," he replied a little grimly. "Now I'm not quite as sure."

"Well, that's not exactly reassuring." Lady Venetia paused at the opening, trying unsuccessfully to remember which path she'd taken before between the tall, obscuring hedges. "But since I already know I'm hopeless and your navigational ability is merely in doubt, you make the decision. Which way—left or right?"

"Left," he said without hesitation, and took her hand.

"Goodness, that was decisive." She smiled up at him, her cheeks pink from the nippy air, her eyes sparkling. He thought she looked enchanting. "No one would suspect that you had no idea where you're going. I hesitate to ask it, but is that the secret of being a good army officer?"

"Giving commands when you've no idea whether or not you've made the right decision? Perhaps. But in this instance I've no reason at all to hesitate."

"You mean you are actually that confident of finding your way?"

"No, I mean I don't actually care whether we get out or not."

Even so, he did manage to guide them, by the expedient of trial and error, through the spiraling half mile of dead ends and open passageways, to the center of the labyrinth.

And once that objective had been realized, it seemed appropriate to celebrate the achievement with a triumphant hug. And once they'd experienced that much intimacy, there seemed no hope of avoiding the kiss that followed and left them both quite devastated.

Lady Venetia gazed up into Major Forbes's face, and the look was stricken. "Please forgive me," she whispered. "I'm entirely to blame. I should never have come here with you. Whatever could I have been thinking of? Oh, what a dreadful coil this is."

Gareth Wincanton could not trust himself to speak. It would not do for him to tell the lady he was falling in love with that the coil she spoke of so feelingly was far, far worse than she could possibly imagine.

Chapter Fourteen

Miss *Amabel Fawnhope's first act upon arriving in* Bath was to visit backstage at the Theatre Royal. It came to her as a bitter disappointment to discover that Nicky was not one of the company there. Indeed, nobody had seen or heard of him. This news had been almost too much to bear, for it made her realize that she was not half so much in pursuit of Gareth Wincanton as in need of the solace Nicky alone could give.

Shame on him, anyway! He could have let her know his change of plans. But how like him. It would never even occur to him that she might worry. Amabel accepted the theory of several of the company personnel that he'd most likely gone to Cheltenham. The touring company there had just lost a romantic lead. Nicky, no doubt, had gotten wind of it.

Her colleagues were sorry for her disappointment, but from the theater's point of view, Miss Fawnhope could not have shown up at a more opportune time. "Providential" was the only word for her unexpected appearance. For the young actress playing Jessica was suffering from the grippe and had lost her voice. Could Amabel not fill the role just for tonight?

Since she'd played the part many times before, it would have been unthinkable for her to refuse. Besides, what difference would one evening make? Perhaps it was just as well that she'd be occupied, for now that she'd run pell-mell to Bath, she was not at all sure what action she should take. She had been relying solely on Nicky's guidance. Now she'd have to think the whole thing through herself.

The counterfeit Major Wincanton had run out of excuses for avoiding the Theatre Royal. So when Sir George Carstairs asked Lady Stoke and her niece and nephew to be his guests for *The Merchant of Venice*, Nicky joined the others in accepting the invitation with every appearance of delight. Then at the first opportunity he hurried off to Beauford Square to inspect the playbill. He breathed a sigh of relief when he did not recognize any of the cast names. Mr. Powell's company had, it seemed, continued on their tour. It should be reasonably safe now for Nicky to attend the performance. No need for a new flare-up of the old war wound.

Still, it was not a festive party that entered the theater box that evening. Venetia had been preoccupied throughout dinner. Also she'd appeared a trifle pale. "Wan" was the word Lady Stoke had used when wondering whether Venetia might be sickening for something. Nicky, after weighing the perils of appearing in public against the awk-wardness of being left alone with his fiancée, had finally chosen the more gentlemanly course. He'd offered to forgo the evening's treat and stay at home with her. But Lady Venetia had reassured them both that her health was excellent.

Even so, for whatever reason, after they'd been seated in the box Sir George had engaged for them, she retained the same listless manner and showed not the slightest interest in quizzing the company as her aunt was busy doing while punctuating her perusal with running comments on this one's jewels and that one's gown.

Nicky, too, was scanning the audience intently, prepared to flee if he saw anyone he knew. He breathed a silent sigh of relief when the only familiar faces he spotted belonged to Lord Piggot-Jones and Mr. St. Leger, who were in a box directly opposite. The only thing he need fear from those two was that his companions might notice that the pair constantly kept their quizzing glasses trained upon their box. Nicky aimed a ferocious scowl across the void that stretched above the occupants of the pit. The two Londoners took the hint and directed their gazes elsewhere.

But when the curtain went up, the professional side of Nicky's nature took over and he became oblivious to everything except the drama taking place onstage. He studied the actors intently, watching bits of business, observing individual techniques for character development. He was especially intent upon the actor playing Shylock and grudgingly acknowledged the genius of Edmund Kean's revolutionary interpretation of that role.

Lady Venetia was also contemplating the art of acting. Not so much as demonstrated upon this stage—she remained for the most part oblivious to the action there—it was the actor's world in general she wondered about, and whether or not Major Nicholas Forbes was connected with that world.

He had denied it vehemently, of course. And she felt almost disloyal in doubting that denial, for Venetia was fairly certain at this point that she was in love with him. But there was no getting around the fact that Major Forbes was a man of mystery.

For one thing, he'd never bothered to explain just how it was that Mr. Powell had come to know him. At this point Venetia took herself in hand. How absurd it was for her to think that actors had no acquaintances outside their own profession. But still, there was no denying that Nicholas Forbes revealed very, very little about himself. Apart from his military career, that is. About that he was quite expansive. Could an actor become an officer? Highly unlikely. But she did wish that his life in England were not such a closed book to her. A sprinkling of polite applause as two new characters took the stage drew Venetia's attention back to the drama unfolding there.

Nicky's had never wavered. He was sitting on the edge of his seat, with his elbows resting on the box rail, when Amabel made her entrance. So absorbed had he become in the dramatic action that this lovely Jessica was merely Shylock's daughter until she spoke. For a moment he froze in horror, unable to believe the testimony of his eyes and ears. Then an instinct for self-preservation took control. He began to quietly inch his chair backward until he was screened by Lady Venetia, who came out of her reverie long enough to glance curiously his way. "May take a nap," he whispered by way of explanation. From his pallor, she wondered if he was feeling pain.

As the play progressed, Nicky gradually relaxed. He was certain now that Amabel had not seen him. If she

138

had, it would be just like her to come dashing around to their box during the interval and stage a family reunion. What the devil was she doing in Bath, anyhow?

The answer, upon reflection, was obvious. Chasing Wincanton, of course. She'd read the *Gazette* announcement. Well, he'd have to see her first thing tomorrow morning and clue her in on his new identity. Nicky flinched as he imagined her reaction. But he couldn't risk doing nothing. The little busybody was bound to manage somehow to let his particular cat out of the bag. He sat back in the shadows and peered over Lady Venetia's shoulder, once more caught up in the action on the stage. God, but Bella was beautiful! And damn good, too. He felt a surge of pride as his eyes followed her.

Amabel's performance was actually a far greater tour de force than Nicholas realized. For she had seen him. And even as she spoke her lines, a part of her attention was fixed upon Sir George Carstairs's box, which she observed from the corner of her eye at every opportunity.

Miss Fawnhope was accustomed to holding her audience spellbound. It had therefore been an affront to her artistry when she'd become aware that a member of that audience was beating a retreat. The fact that she'd managed to hide the shock of discovery when her eyes, still in character, had traveled in that direction was a tribute to the stern discipline of her art. And the fact that she was able to keep the box under surveillance without revealing that she did so was a second testimonial.

After her initial identification of the gentleman, whose red hair alone was now visible, Amabel had paid little attention to him. Having finally located Gareth Wincanton was enough. It was his fiancée who now claimed all her interest. By the time Amabel made her final exit she had memorized Lady Venetia's every feature.

As soon as the curtain came down, Nicky rushed his party out of the theater. When Lady Stoke protested this unseemly haste, his excuse was to get a jump on the other patrons and avoid the crush. But since Sir George's coachman had not felt the same compunction and was well back in the long line of carriages queued to pick up their owners, they were forced to stand around for several minutes with Nicky glancing repeatedly and surreptitiously over his shoulder.

It was a close thing. He was handing the ladies inside the carriage when he heard a voice trill, "Oh, Major Wincanton!"

The little gudgeon had mistaken him! Well, she wouldn't do so for long, and he couldn't rely on tipping her the wink. Nicky gave Sir George a quick shove that almost landed him in Louisa's lap, then hissed "Spring 'em!" at the driver as he leaped into the coach himself.

This order was impossible to execute, due to the crush of traffic, but they did begin to move away at a pace sufficient to halt Miss Fawnhope in her tracks.

" 'Pon my soul, I believe that little actress was hailing you," Sir George observed, looking back in her direction through his quizzing glass.

"How odd." Lady Stoke craned her neck to see. "Do you know her, Win?"

"Never saw her before in my life," Nicky observed virtuously. "Couldn't've been me she was after. You must've mistaken the matter, sir."

"Oh, to be sure, I must have." Sir George Carstairs, man of the world, awoke suddenly to the fact that he'd been most tactless and tried to rectify his gaffe. "Come to think of it, I do believe that 'Will Canton' was the name she shouted. 'Will Canton' sounds much like Wincanton, don't you know. Some chap in the carriage just behind us, I've no doubt.''

''Hmmm'' was Lady Stoke's reaction.

Lady Venetia, though, made no comment at all. She'd missed the entire episode. Her thoughts were clearly elsewhere.

Chapter Fifteen

Despite his resolve to see Amabel early next morning, Nicky Forbes slept late.

The actress and Lady Venetia did not. They both were up betimes, and both appeared in the Pump Room at eleven o'clock.

Miss Fawnhope's objective was to consult the guest list and see if Major Wincanton had entered his direction. Lady Venetia, who had announced her intention of going for a walk, had been entrusted to carry a message there for Lady Stoke.

Venetia was seated at a table with its recipient, a dowager who sipped mineral water while holding her nose, when she grew aware that she was under scrutiny. It took her a moment to realize that the lovely young lady staring at her was the actress who had played the part of Jessica the night before.

As Venetia took her leave of her aunt's friend and crossed the room, the actress accosted her. "Lady Venetia Lowther, I believe?" Amabel inquired.

Venetia, puzzled but polite, acknowledged her identity.

"My name is Miss Fawnhope." Amabel's accents were aristocratic to a fault. "There is something I think I should tell you."

Just why Venetia was suddenly afraid that the actress's business had to do with Nicholas Forbes defied all reason. No one knew of that association except her and Nicholas. At least they did not unless Nicholas had told them. This much she was certain of: whatever the beauty wished to confide was bound to be unpleasant.

As the two faced each other across a table that commanded a view of the patrons clustered around the pump, Amabel was beginning to lose some of her self-assurance. Ever since she'd read of Major Wincanton's betrothal, she'd had but one thought in mind—to pay him back for his shabby treatment. Revenge, as she'd pictured it, would be sweet indeed. The problem was that while it would be one thing to grind Wincanton into the dust, exacting vengeance upon this polite young lady, with her troubled eyes, was not the same thing at all. Still, what other course was available? Amabel scotched her scruples and came directly to the point.

"You and I, Lady Venetia, have something in common, it seems. Major Wincanton."

"Gareth?" Venetia was unaware that she sounded relieved. "I'm sorry, but I can't recall that he has mentioned you."

"It ain't—isn't likely that he has. It would not be 'gen-

143

tlemanly.' And before all else, Gareth's a gentleman."
Amabel was warming to her work now, her anger rekindling. "He would not consider it at all the thing to tell his fiancée that while he was offering her marriage he was offering a carte blanche to me."

Venetia was too stunned to speak. Her face drained of color. Amabel felt a pang of sympathy, which she quickly suppressed. "I—I don't believe you," Lady Venetia finally managed to say.

Amabel shrugged and rose, anxious to put the interview to an end. Things were not going at all the way she'd imagined. Damn Wincanton, anyhow. Why was it always the females who did the suffering? "You don't have to believe me unless you wish to." Her voice was pitying. "I just thought you ought to know."

She'd taken several steps away when Lady Venetia called after her, "Wait, Miss Fawnhope. There's something I'd like to ask you." As Amabel turned inquiringly, Venetia lowered her voice. "You're in the theater. Have you ever heard of an actor called Nicholas Forbes?"

"Nicholas Forbes? Why, yes, of course. I should say I have! Don't tell me that you actually know Nicky!"

"Oh, no. I don't know him. I don't actually know him at all. The name just came up recently, and I was curious. Just curious, that's all. Thank you for enlightening me."

Amabel was at a loss to understand why this puzzling conversation seemed to have upset her ladyship even more than the news of her fiancé's infidelity had.

Major Gareth Wincanton thought it might possibly have been the worst moment of his life. After strolling across the street from the White Hart, he had looked in on the Pump Room, where his eyes riveted upon Lady Venetia Lowther and Miss Amabel Fawnhope deep in conversa-

144

tion. For an instant he had stood immobilized. But military tactician that he was, he soon rallied his forces to beat a hasty, if inglorious, retreat.

Once safely out of the line of sight of the two females who, in entirely different ways, had turned his life upside-down, he broke into a cold and clammy sweat. Together, they were bound to bring about his total ruin. Every instinct told him to lose no time in racing back to his rooms, packing his boxes, and haring off to London. But like some doomed classical tragic figure, Wincanton seemed incapable of avoiding the inexorable unfolding of his fate.

Instead, he stood lurking in the Abbey churchyard, watching the Pump Room door. As Miss Fawnhope made her exit and hurried off in the direction of the theater, he stepped behind a pillar of the colonnade. But when Lady Venetia emerged, some minutes later, the major took one look at her stricken face and promptly lost his self-preservation instinct. He squared his shoulders, set his jaw, left off skulking, and went to intercept her.

As for Venetia, she found nothing strange at all in the fact that Nicholas Forbes had suddenly materialized, taken her elbow, and was guiding her toward the Abbey grounds. They climbed the steps leading to the terrace, then went to stand by a stone wall and stare sightlessly at the Avon. He gave her a few minutes to compose herself before he asked huskily, "Can you tell me about it?"

"I shouldn't. You'll think I'm making far too much of the whole business." She spoke so softly that he was forced to stoop to hear it. "Everyone did before. A lady is supposed to overlook that sort of thing. Indeed, not even to know it. But I don't think I could ever learn to share my husband. Especially"—her voice was bitter—"always knowing that I was second choice. I'm proud, you see."

"You could never be second choice."

"You think not?" Her smile was self-mocking. "Then you'll be amazed to learn that I only have to become promised to someone to discover he keeps a harem."

At that point they were joined by a group of sightseers exploring the Abbey and its grounds. "Let's go," he said. They walked down the steps in a silence that persisted until they reached the Orange Grove. "I don't see any oranges anywhere." He glanced pointedly at the trees, trying to lighten her mood a bit.

"It's named for the Prince of Orange, not the fruit." She managed a wan smile as he led her to a bench that faced the promenade.

"You'll have to explain the 'harem' remark," he said, prodding gently.

She was under better control now. But she pulled a handkerchief from her reticule, dabbed at her eyes to discourage any tears that might lurk there, then twisted the tiny square of linen with nervous fingers. "Well, I was rather indulging in hyperbole," she admitted. "There's no such thing as a one-woman harem, is there? But the lowering truth is, I've been promised in marriage twice, and in both instances it's been my bad luck to discover that my fiancé is in love with someone else."

"You mean there was someone else before Ni—before Major Wincanton?"

Venetia, fortunately, was too steeped in misery to notice the slip. "Oh, yes. I was betrothed to someone I knew in Spain. We were considered the 'perfect couple.' Only he had fixed his interest elsewhere." Wincanton listened with increasing foreboding as she went on to describe the shock and revulsion she'd felt upon learning that the gentleman she was supposed to marry had already established an out-of-wedlock household.

146

"But surely he would have given up his mistress."

"Oh, he said as much. Though I've every reason to believe he loved her. But then you'd be amazed at the sacrifices one is willing to make for a fortune. I was not so heartless as to demand it of him, however. You see, I'd also discovered that his mistress was *enceinte*. I could hardly condone abandoning an expectant mother. Though to give him credit, I never thought for an instant that he would."

"Oh, my God," Wincanton groaned. He waited for a group of strollers to pass and then observed, "But surely yours is a case of 'once burned, twice shy,' is it not? I can't believe that your Major Wincanton has that sort of arrangement."

"Indeed, he hasn't." She laughed bitterly. "But not from want of trying. You see, I've just had a very enlightening interview with a Miss Amabel Fawnhope, who told me that while Major Wincanton was pursuing me with a view toward matrimony, he was offering her a most generous carte blanche."

"That sounds a bit improbable," he observed weakly. "I mean to say, when could he have found the time?"

"You think she's lying, then?" She clutched the straw and then abandoned it. "Well, I do not. Not for a moment. As to how he managed, she didn't say. Perhaps he wrote after our betrothal was announced. Anyway, 'how' has nothing to say in the matter. For I'm sure she told the truth. Also, I'm sure it's Miss Fawnhope he really wants. What gentleman would not? She's a diamond of the first water. I doubt I've seen a more bewitching creature."

"You could not have looked in your glass, then."

"That's gallant of you, Nicholas. But it's also fustian. I've no illusions. I simply have to resign myself to the fact that among females of my class, marriages of convenience are the rule and not the exception—and that gentlemen fall in love with women of quite another stamp.''

"Now, that really *is* fustian," he said savagely. "You should not jump to such daft conclusions. My God, you haven't even given Wincanton the chance to defend himself. Most likely he doesn't love this woman at all.''

"You wouldn't say that if you'd seen her.''

"Oh, wouldn't I? Well, for the sake of argument, let's admit that she's all you say. 'Bewitching' was the term you used, was it not? But you surely must know, Venetia, that a man can desire a woman without having his heart involved. It's not much of a testimonial for my sex, I'll grant you, but there it is. Could you not give your major the benefit of the doubt?''

"Oh, but I do." She took a deep, shuddering breath, trying to hold back the tears that were threatening to flow. "Not in the way you mean, perhaps, but you'd be amazed at how much more sympathetic I am with Gareth than I ever was with Fletcher, my first fiancé. You see, Nicholas, I've no trouble at all now in seeing how it can so easily happen—to fall in love with the wrong sort of person entirely, I mean.''

He was at a total loss now, with no idea what to say. "That's most broad-minded of you," he ventured.

"I know. I can scarcely believe it of myself. Why, I've even developed a certain appreciation for the institution of carte blanche. What a pity it is that ladies haven't the opportunity to make the same sort of arrangements that gentlemen do. But now I am being absurd." The tears suddenly spilled over.

Wincanton took her in his arms. "Don't cry, Venetia. Please don't cry, my darling. This can all be straightened out. I'm sure of it. I'd stake my life that Wincanton doesn't really love that actress.''

"Oh, but it's not Gareth that I'm crying for. How could you even think so? It's not his deception that's destroyed me. It's yours. Oh, Nicholas, why did you have to lie to me? Why could you not simply have admitted from the start that you're an actor? If I had known, why, then— perhaps, just possibly—I could have walked away before I came to love you."

Chapter Sixteen

*N*icky went first to the theater to discover Amabel's direction. Then, as he sauntered the short distance to her Queen Square lodging house, he wasn't overly concerned that he had overslept. Bella was not noted for early rising at any time, and after a performance it was her habit to lie in bed till noon. He was therefore amazed to learn from a rather starchy landlady named Mrs. Massey that Miss Fawnhope had gone out. ''As to where she's gone,'' the woman replied to Nicky's probing, ''I really couldn't say.''

It took considerable persuasion on his part, laced with considerable more charm, for the landlady to finally allow Nicky to come inside and wait. She did not as a rule rent to theatrical people, she'd explained, but since her previous tenant had left unexpectedly and Miss Fawnhope was only temporary, she had made this one exception. But the inference was clear. There'd be no "goings-on" within her premises. It was only when Nicky explained that he was Miss Fawnhope's brother that he gained access to a small and shabby parlor. Mrs. Massey's sniff had made it clear that while she didn't accept this spurious kinship for a moment, it would do for any neighbors who might be peeping through the curtains across the way.

The waiting seemed interminable. It had come to him as a relief the night before, albeit an awkward one, when Amabel had shouted "Wincanton" after him, instead of "Nicky." But now he wondered if she could have gone looking for the major this morning and been told she'd find that gentleman at Lansdown Circle. Just as his anxiety reached alarming heights, the front door opened and he heard her footsteps in the hall.

Amabel glanced into the parlor, then went rigid. But her initial hostile look turned quickly to astonishment and then delight. "Nicky! I thought you were Wincanton!" She rushed across the room and flung herself into his arms. "Oh, Nicky, Nicky darling, I'm so glad to see you." She reached up to peck him on the cheek. The caress was intercepted by his quicker lips. The intensity and duration of the ensuing kiss would have certainly cast considerable doubt on his fraternal status if the landlady had happened to be watching.

"Oh, Nicky," Amabel said rather breathlessly when he finally released her, "you're a sight for sore eyes. You really are. But wherever have you sprung from? I thought you must be in Cheltenham."

"No, I've been here all along, Bella. But it's a complicated story. And I think you'd best sit down to hear it."

They shared Mrs. Massey's unyielding sofa as Nicky poured out the story of the wager and of all the ensuing complications that bit of drunken folly had brought on.

Amabel was a good listener. She gasped aloud occasionally, her lovely eyes grew even wider, but she did not speak till he was finished.

"Let me see if I have this straight, then. Gareth is not really engaged to Lady Venetia. You are."

"In a manner of speaking, that's right. Though, of course, when she learns—"

She clapped a hand across his mouth. "Oh, please, don't say a word yet. My head is spinning. Let's see, now. Lady Venetia became betrothed to Major Gareth Wincanton, who is really you. And now Major Wincanton has come to town, pretending to be Nicholas Forbes."

"Well, that was not actually his intention. To pose as me, I mean. Venetia simply jumped to that conclusion when she met him, because she knew through a chance meeting we had with Mr. Powell—he was playing Claudius here, you know, but now his troupe's moved on to Nottingham. Anyhow, he said he mistook me for someone else, so she knew that there was a cove loose somewhere who looked like me; ergo, she—"

"Nicky!" Amabel's tone was almost a shriek. "Will you stop it? I don't think I can bear any more. It's all too utterly improbable. Like one of those dreadful comedies of William Shakespeare where everybody is really somebody else."

"Well, at least Wincanton and I are the same sex," Nicky said defensively. "But forget my tangle for a while and tell me why you're here. Not that I can't guess. You saw the notice in the *Gazette*. Am I right?"

"Yes, I came to have it out with Gareth." She looked quite ferocious.

"Did you mind so terribly much, Bella? That he was going to be married, I mean."

"Mind? I was furious. Do you know what kind of offer he made *me,* Nicky? Two thousand pounds a year and a house. That's the kind of offer he made me!"

This time *his* eyes widened. He gave a long, low whistle. "Two thousand pounds plus a house? So what did you tell him, Bella?"

"Why, to go to the devil, of course. *I'm* not good enough for a marriage offer, Nicky." Her eyes filled with tears; whether of hurt or rage, he'd no notion.

"I know I've asked before, but did you love him, Bella?"

"Oh, how should I know? I suppose I did. Well, perhaps I didn't. But I wanted him to propose marriage. That I am sure of."

"Well, if you didn't love the man, the devil with him." He put a brotherly arm around her, and she snuggled up against his shoulder. "I know I shouldn't say it, Bella, but I'm glad about the way it all turned out. My reason tells me you've probably been a fool, but there it is. I'm still glad you didn't accept Wincanton's offer of carte blanche."

"The carte blanche!" Amabel sat up suddenly and turned a horrified gaze upon him. "I had forgotten! The carte blanche! Oh, my heavens! I've really loosed the cat among the pigeons!"

"What are you ranting about now, for God's sake, Bella?"

"Oh, Nicky, I've done the most dreadful thing," she wailed. "I've just told Lady Venetia that at the same time you were pursuing her with marriage in mind, you were planning to live a life of sin with me."

* * *

Lady Stoke was waiting to waylay Nicky on his return to the Crescent. She appeared much agitated. "Something dreadful's happened to Venetia" were her first words. "I've never seen her in such a state. She's locked in her room and won't open the door to me. You see if you can discover what the matter is, Win dear."

But when he tapped softly on Venetia's door, a muffled voice replied, "Please go away."

"It's me, Venetia. We need to talk."

"Not now."

"Yes, now. I know what's bothering you, and I can explain. Do you wish me to do it from out here for everyone to hear?" He looked pointedly at the upstairs maid, who turned brick-red and began vigorously polishing the table she was poised over.

The key turned in the lock. Nicky opened it and went inside while Venetia once more threw herself, facedown, upon her bed. He pulled up a chair, for all the world like an attending physician, and reached for her hand. She quickly jerked it away.

"Be reasonable, Venetia. We can't talk like this. Please, look at me."

He was almost sorry he'd insisted, for when she did sit up and prop herself against the pillows, her face was tear-stained and puffy-eyed, altogether quite pathetically heart-wrenching.

"I don't know where to begin." He would not have been half so conscience-stricken if he were guilty merely of the thing she believed he was. "I know that Bella—Miss Fawn-hope, I mean to say—has talked to you. But what I'm afraid of is that you're taking it the wrong way entirely, looking at the situation in the worst possible light, that is."

Nicky ran his fingers through his hair in desperation, unconsciously making a hash of its artful Titus arrange-

154

ment. He was acutely conscious though of the hash he was making of the conversation. But how the deuce to proceed? Above all things, he wanted Lady Venetia to call off their betrothal, but he certainly didn't wish to crush her in the process. Just when she'd finally recovered from the blow of discovering that one fiancé had a mistress of long standing, she'd been planted a leveler a second time. How *used* she must be feeling. Of a sudden his concern took precedence over his instinct for survival.

"You mustn't get the wrong idea," he floundered on, "the way you did with that other cove you were engaged to. You seemed to come away from that business thinking that the only possible reason any man would marry you is for your fortune." He held up a hand to forestall any comment she might make. "Please, hear me out. This ain't easy, you see, since I'm in the wrong of it. I just want you to know that I agree it's right and proper you should break off our engagement. If I were you, I'd do it in a flash. What's not right and proper is for you to keep clinging to the notion that you ain't up to snuff where the opposite sex is concerned. What I mean to say is, you're one of the most desirable females I've ever met."

There was no doubting his sincerity. Venetia's eyes were fixed upon his face. She scarcely breathed.

"That was the problem, don't you see. Not the other way around." He suddenly grew inspired. "I haven't played you false. It was Amabel—Miss Fawnhope—I betrayed. Our attachment was of long standing, you see, and the last thing I'd intended was to get involved with any other female. But then you and I got caught in the storm that day. And then you slipped. And there I was, holding you. Well, you know what happened. God's truth, I couldn't help myself. But I am sorry, sorrier than I can ever manage to express, that I've put you through all this.

I know it must be something of a trial, having to keep calling engagements off. But you mustn't let it sour you on romance. The right man will come along for you. I'm sure of it. You know what they always say—third time lucky."

There was a long, pregnant silence. Nicky squirmed uneasily in his chair as Venetia continued to study him. She applied the sodden handkerchief she'd been twisting to her nose and then blew vigorously. The action seemed to bring resolve.

"Do you plan to marry her?" she asked.

"Bella, you mean?"

"I mean Miss Fawnhope. She's the mistress under discussion, isn't she? Tell me. Are there others?"

"Of course not." He was stung.

"Well, then. Do you plan to marry her?"

Nicky was having trouble keeping his personae straight. He had to remind himself that he was Major Gareth Wincanton, toffee-nosed snob. "N-no. I don't think I can do that. Wouldn't be the thing. An actress, don't you know."

Tears welled once more into her eyes, much to his consternation. "Yes, I can see that marriage under those circumstances is quite unthinkable." She took a deep, shuddery breath. "Well, then, that's that. There's no need to break off our engagement."

"Oh, I say! You can't be serious!"

Venetia interpreted Nicky's expression as amazement at her broad-mindedness. It would have been nearer to the mark to say he was aghast.

"Oh, I'm quite serious. If you don't intend to marry the woman you love, there's no reason you shouldn't marry me. It will be a splendid match in the eyes of the world. It will please our families. And we should deal quite well together."

"Oh, no, we wouldn't. What I mean to say is, you mustn't. Damn it all, Venetia, you have to break off our engagement. You can't have that sort of marriage. You were right in the first place when you booted out that other cove. You deserve much better."

"No"—she sighed deeply—"that's just what I don't deserve." Her resolve stiffened. "You've been open with me, Gareth. Now it's my turn to be honest. You see, I've come to understand just what it means to fall in love with someone entirely unsuitable."

"You have?" He looked skeptical.

"Oh, yes. It's true. And it's quite ironic, really. You're in love with an actress. I've fallen in love with an actor. So now you can see why I should make you the perfect wife." She laughed shakily. "I doubt that many couples have quite so much in common."

"You—Lady Venetia Lowther—a viscount's daughter—in love with an actor?" His jaw dropped. "I'll not believe it."

"And why not?" she countered. "You, Major Gareth Wincanton, grandson of an earl, in love with an actress? What's sauce for the gander, you know."

"But who? When? Why?" he sputtered. "My word, surely not Mr. Powell! I know he's elegant—could pass for a toff any day—does, in fact—typecast in all those king-duke-knight roles. But he's old enough to be your father."

"Of course it's not Mr. Powell. Don't be absurd. I don't even know him."

"Well, who, then?"

She sighed deeply. "Does it matter?"

"Of course it matters!"

"Well, if you must know. You may remember my mentioning that I'd met your look-alike. Well, I've seen him a few times since then. And I'd simply assumed he was a

157

gentleman, you see. But then, well, just today—from your Miss Fawnhope, to be exact—I've discovered that he's an *actor*." The term *highwayman* would have sounded less distasteful.

Nicky stared transfixed, convinced his ears had just deceived him. "Now, let me get this straight." He spoke slowly, deliberately. "You're telling me that you've actually fallen in love with Major—I mean to say, with an *actor* named Nicholas Forbes?"

Her face flamed. "Well, I collect he actually is a major. I didn't think to ask Miss Fawnhope about—" She did not conclude her sentence. Her listener was doubled up with laughter.

"I really can't see why you find the situation so amusing," she said icily when he'd somewhat recovered and was wiping his streaming eyes. "I certainly did not develop a case of the whoops when I learned of your attachment to Miss Fawnhope."

"No, no. You mustn't take offense. You don't understand." His shoulders began to shake again, but under the influence of her glare he managed a tolerable state of sobriety. "It's just that here you are, enacting this Cheltenham tragedy about loving an actor— By the by, you wouldn't consider actually marrying one, would you? No? Well, I always thought as much. Love doesn't conquer all, now, does it, and the cove who thought that one up must've had maggots on the brain.

"I'm sorry. I realize I'm straying from the point a bit. But what I'm getting at is, there's no need to put yourself into such a taking. It's quite all right for you to be in love with him. For he ain't the actor, you see. I am— Oh, my God!"

Nicholas slapped his forehead, appalled at what he'd just let slip. "I've sunk the wager." He groaned piteously, then slumped down in his armchair, his head leaning for support against the carved top rail. "What a chivalrous imbecile I've turned out to be," he muttered hoarsely. "Don Quixote couldn't begin to touch me for mutton-headedness."

Venetia, on the other hand, had lost the last vestige of her earlier lethargy and had no tolerance for his. She came leaping out of bed to stand over him and barely restrained herself from seizing his shoulders and giving him a shake. "What do you mean Nicholas isn't the actor, you are?"

"Nothing. Nothing at all. Just got carried away there for a minute. Pay no attention to my ravings. It's been a trying day."

But Venetia's brain was racing, piecing together peculiar bits of conversation and certain odd behaviors that at the time she'd dismissed as merely eccentric. Now she pounced on the obvious conclusion. "You *are* Nicholas Forbes, aren't you, Win? Just like the man in Molland's pastry shop said you were. He had it right all along. You're Nicholas Forbes, the actor!" Venetia fairly crowed in the triumph of discovery.

"No need to shout it to the housetops," he protested in a whisper that he hoped would set the tone. "But yes, you're right, of course. I'm Forbes."

She sat back down on the edge of the bed, feeling suddenly a bit weak-kneed as the full implication of his admission struck her. "Then who—?"

"Major Gareth Wincanton, who else?" came the bitter answer.

"But I don't understand." The fact that she was whispering had more to do with failing breath than his example.

"I know you don't." He sighed. "I'm about to explain it to you."

And for the second time that day, he launched into a recital of the harebrained wager, this time tactfully skirting around the real reason for Wincanton's reluctance to leave town. It was a story that didn't improve much with the telling. It seemed to lack that certain edifying moral example that always makes a tale well worth repeating. But it held his audience. No doubt of that. Lady Venetia hung on his every word.

"So it was all just a drunken bet, then," she summed up at its conclusion.

"That's right. And I've just lost it."

He slumped in dejected silence, with closed eyes, trying to think of some way he might possibly pay off the wager. Bella could be good for a touch. No! The devil with that idea. He'd just have to run for it. That's what gentlemen did when their debts piled up: took a packet out of Dover for the Continent. Lived in exile.

Nicky cut short these morbid thoughts. After all, what did it matter? He squared his shoulders. It was a splendid thing that he'd just done. He'd always been a soft touch when it came to women's tears. A pretty woman's, anyhow. Why count the personal cost? He'd made Venetia happy. He opened his eyes wide then, wishing to imprint Venetia's glow of happiness upon his memory, to call it back to mind during the bleak days of his exile abroad. But Lady Venetia was not glowing. She looked, in fact, like a storm about to break.

"Oh, I say." Nicky could not help sounding a bit aggrieved at this improper response to his chivalric self-destruction. "I don't think you quite get the picture yet, Lady Venetia. You're in love with the right cove after all. There's absolutely no social barrier between you and your *amour propre*. Things couldn't be jollier."

"Oh, no?" she said between clenched teeth. "Well, if

that's your opinion, you can't be thinking properly. Hasn't it occurred to you that if *you're* Nicholas Forbes and *he's* Major Gareth Wincanton, then *he's* the one who made the offer of carte blanche to that—that—actress? You may think the situation's jolly, but I say that history's odious habit of repeating itself has gone entirely too far this time!"

Chapter
Seventeen

"*B*otheration!" was Lady Stoke's reaction to the butler's announcement that her carriage was waiting. "Send it away, Hope. No, wait. I can't do that. Lady Mansfield would never forgive me if I left her one short at cards. Come ride with me, Win—oh, *Nicholas*, I should say, though I vow I'll never get used to the matter. Do come along, m'dear. We don't have time to waste, and I wish to tell you what's best to be done."

Nicky's opinion of Lady Stoke had always been high. Even so, it had soared in the past half hour. She had listened to his confession, made at Lady Venetia's insistence, with a breathless interest that was totally devoid of disapproval. "I vow it's better than a play," she'd pronounced at the conclusion of his recital. "And though I was completely taken in, I must say I'm not at all surprised."

Nicky had long since ceased trying to follow her ladyship's forays into the realm of logic. "You're not?" he asked.

"Not in the least. I remember thinking it was a miracle that any member of the Wincanton family could have your looks and charm."

Nicky tried to look modest and did not succeed.

"And then there were things about you that, well . . . did not seem quite right. Can't put me finger on anything specific, but as I recall now, certain things that you did and said surprised me."

"Not quite the gentleman, I collect."

"No, that wasn't it." Her ladyship was quick to restore Nicky's pride of performance. "Come to think of it, you may have been a bit too much the gentleman. Still, that's merely hindsight, I expect. Wait—now I know what it was that seemed a bit off target. You're too likable by half. And Wincanton as a boy always kept himself to himself. I just concluded that the war had changed him. But then, I doubt that being shot at would make a person more agreeable. At least, I never heard of it."

Now, as they emerged from the house, Nicky saw Jocko Hodges standing in the street by the horses, while Lady Stoke's coachman waited in the driver's seat. His heart sank. "I think we should wait to finish our discussion," he whispered as he handed her ladyship into the barouche while the tiger ran around to take his place as postilion in the rumble.

"Nonsense!" her ladyship replied in her usual carrying tones. "We haven't time to waste. That's why I wanted you to ride with me, remember? The thing is, I wished to speak to you about the wager.''

With effort Nicky repressed a groan. Experience had taught him it would do no good for him to try to point out the proximity of the tiger. As far as Lady Stoke was concerned, servants possessed no ears. Nicholas knew better. He could actually hear Jocko's snap to attention.

''What I wish to say is this. Just because you've told Venetia and me who you really are, there's no need to make confession a habit. I'll speak to her as soon as I get home. I'm positive that once she's cooled down a bit she'll see your side of the thing. After all, you're out of work and need the money. My only regret is that Wincanton himself won't be losing a bundle. He should get his comeuppance for playing such a shabby trick on me.'' Her eyes flashed with indignation. ''Well, anyway, I don't see why you should be the one to suffer. So I'm confident that I can persuade Venetia to continue our charade for two days longer. By then your time will be up and you can collect your little nest egg. Yes, by heaven, the more I think of it, the more I'm convinced that there's absolutely no need for you to tell those scoundrels you've been found out. Well, what do you say?''

''Oh, I couldn't agree more, your ladyship,'' Nicky replied hollowly. ''There's absolutely no need for me to say anything at all.''

Behind them, the tiger cleared his throat significantly.

Two hours later Mr. Nicholas Forbes entered the portals of the White Hart in compliance with a summons he'd received from Mr. Bertram St. Leger and Owen, Lord Piggot-Jones. A casual observer would have thought he hadn't a care in the world. He was dapperly dressed, in a coat of cerulean blue adorned with large brass buttons. Biscuit pantaloons hugged his well-shaped thighs and calves. His Hessians shone with champagne blacking; their golden tassels added to the gleam. He wore his curly-brimmed beaver at a cocky angle that exposed one side of his fiery hair. Heads turned admiringly as he proceeded up the stairs.

Even as he raised his hand to knock on Wincanton's door, it opened. A servant ushered him into the room, then silently departed. Four empty chairs were placed in a semicircle before the fireplace. St. Leger, Piggot-Jones, and Wincanton were standing with their backs to the glowing coals, a solemn tribunal, staring his way. The Sprig nodded coolly, and Nicky tipped his hat in answer, then laid it, along with his soft kid gloves and silver-handled stick, upon a Pembroke table by the door. He and Gareth Wincanton deliberately avoided each other's eyes.

He took the chair that St. Leger gestured toward, stretched out his legs, and crossed them, trying to appear nonchalant for the benefit of the gentry coves while at the same time attempting to dispel a growing feeling that he was being court-martialed—an eventuality he'd always considered a distinct possibility during his army days. That notion retreated a bit when St. Leger thrust a brandy in his hand. He doubted the army would be that considerate.

"We asked you here to explain yourself." Lord Piggot-Jones threw down the gauntlet as the others took their seats.

Nicky sampled his cognac deliberately, then shrugged. "There's nothing to explain. I made a good run of it, but the jig's up now. They know who I really am."

"They know because you told them!" the Sprig accused, his voice rising in indignation. "Wincanton's tiger heard you admit it. Of all the unprincipled, underhanded, unsporting— But then, what could you expect?'' he finished bitterly. ''It all comes of punting with a Cit. Should've known you'd have no proper notion of correct behavior.''

''Well, then, that's that.'' Nicky smiled pleasantly at his hosts and set his glass on the candle stand near his elbow. ''Seems there's no more to be said. I'll be on my way.''

''The devil you will!'' The Sprig jumped up to plant himself between Nicky and the door. The action seemed rather ill-advised, since Nicky topped him by at least six inches. ''By God, you owe us an explanation.''

''By God, I owe you nothing.''

''I wouldn't go quite so far as that, old man,'' Piggot-Jones observed. ''As a matter of fact, you owe me a thousand pounds.''

''Well, I for one ain't too sure of that.'' The Sprig glared at his lordship, taking up an argument that had raged before Nicky's arrival. ''I still say it's all Wincanton's doing. For I'll bet a monkey he's the one that caused Nicky here to have to blow the gab. Wincanton violated the terms of our wager by coming to Bath, and that's a fact. And I'm blessed if I'm going to pay up till I find out what's what.

''So look here, Nicky, old man, come down off your high ropes and be reasonable.'' His tone had shifted to cajolery. ''If there was a good reason for you doing what you did, I think you should say so. You ain't in no better position than I am to cough up all that blunt.''

''The difference is, he's no intention of paying up,'' Piggot-Jones observed as he breathed on his quizzing glass and then polished it.

''That was a knavish thing to say.'' Major Wincanton made his first contribution to the conversation, and Piggot-

Jones quailed before his stare. "You owe Forbes an apology."

"Sorry, old man. Don't know what came over me." His lordship smiled weakly in the actor's direction.

Nicky, who had been stung by Piggot-Jones's words despite their accuracy, nodded his way stiffly.

"Oh, do sit back down, Nicky," the Sprig implored, "and let's talk this thing out like gentlemen." He colored then as Nicky gave him a speaking look.

The actor did resume his chair, however, for upon sober reflection he was of the Sprig's frame of mind—it would be far better to nullify the wager than to decamp for the Continent. He started to sip his brandy, then set it down, perhaps remembering the folly of drinking too deep in his present company.

The Sprig assumed the role of barrister. "Now, Nicky, all I ask is that you tell us *why* you told Lady Venetia Lowther that you ain't Wincanton here."

There was a protracted pause while Nicky concentrated on the question. "Oh, lord, who knows," he finally said, sighing. He had already spent considerable time pondering that same conundrum without giving himself any satisfactory answer. So what hope had he of satisfying the Sprig? "Maybe I was just getting stale in the role. It does happen that way sometimes, you know." He squirmed a bit as St. Leger looked murderous. "Oh, the devil with it, then. I don't really know why. I collect it may have happened because I never could stand to see a female cry. Don't ask me to explain why that should be. For all of 'em are able to turn on their fountains at the slightest excuse. And it works with me every time. And, of course, the young and pretty ones are the worst when it comes to oversetting a chap. And the ones like Lady Venetia, who ain't usually prone to that sort of thing, really get under my skin. So I

167

guess that's as close to a reason I can come up with for telling her who I really am. She was unhappy, and I wanted to make her feel better. It didn't work," he concluded with more than a trace of bitterness. "But I wasn't to know that, was I?"

For the first time, Gareth Wincanton was looking fully at his impersonator. He studied Nicky's face intently while the actor contemplated the untouched liquid in his glass. The room was silent.

"Well, for God's sake, man." The Sprig was finally forced to act as prompter. "You've got to go on and tell us why Lady Venetia was crying and why the deuce knowing who you really are would make her stop it."

"No. I've not got to tell you anything." Nicky gave him a level look. "I may only be a Cit, but I don't discuss a lady's private affairs."

"But dammit, we've got to know if it had anything at all to do with Wincanton showing up here in Bath, and I still say it's bound to have. She must have thought about it and figured out what's what. Or somebody else saw him and told her who he was. That's likely, too. But one way or another, his being here is bound to have tipped the scales. And all I need is a little proof of that. Then I say the wager's null and void. And I'll take it up with the membership at Brooks' if I have to before I pay!"

"St. Leger, that's enough!" Major Gareth Wincanton, late of His Majesty's Household Brigade, was accustomed to instilling the fear of God into his army subalterns. It worked on civilians, too. The Sprig subsided. "The devil take your wager. I'm sick of hearing of it. You've made your point. I should never have come to Bath. More than that, I should never have agreed to the impersonation. But what's done's done. I'll pay off the damned bet. But on one condition—that you give me your solemn word, St.

168

Leger, never to mention this business to anyone again, especially me.''

"Oh, but I say!'' Lord Piggot-Jones yelped in protest, leaping to his feet. "You can't do that. I won. Fair and square.''

"Oh, stow it, Owen. I mean to pay you off, as well. Same conditions: forget that all this happened.'' Wincanton strode over to the writing table, found pen, ink, and paper, and scratched vigorously while the three men stared in silence. "Here.'' He thrust three sheets of paper into their hands. "Just present these to my banker. Now then, I trust we can consider this whole shoddy episode at an end.''

St. Leger and Piggot-Jones glanced at their notes. Their eyes widened, and they quickly pocketed them. Nicky frowned down at his long enough to see that the major had actually increased the amount he would have won. A smile slowly lighted up his countenance, culminating in an impish grin. Then, while Wincanton watched with narrowed eyes, Nicholas Forbes, impoverished actor, ripped the paper in two with a broad, dramatic flourish. After that, unsatisfied with this piece of business, he went on to shred the sections into minute pieces and fling them in the air.

"Damned generous of you, but I'm afraid I can't take your blunt, old boy.'' He looked Wincanton steadily in the eye. "Don't seem right to take payment for playing such a shabby trick on two lovely ladies. Besides, I couldn't accept money for the best hospitality of my life. Not quite the thing, don't you know.'' His grin grew wider as the other dropped his gaze.

Nicholas Forbes clapped his stylish beaver perilously near one eyebrow and picked up his cane and gloves. As he paused in the doorway to break his exit, his bow was mocking. "Good day, *gentlemen*."

Edmund Kean, star of Drury Lane, could not have touched the irony Nicky packed into his final word.

Chapter
Eighteen

*N*icky exited the White Hart, still limping. Then, as it occurred to him that the encumbering bit of characterization was no longer needed, he stepped out jauntily, swinging his cane in an exaggerated rhythm with his steps. He even whistled a stirring marching tune.

His glow lasted all the way down Milsom to George Street before a reaction set in. The whistling slowed down, then trailed off altogether. His cane ceased to swing and rested in his arm crook. His step faltered. Before he knew it, he'd resumed his limp. Finally, he berated himself for a damned, quixotic fool.

What had come over him, anyhow? He had used to be so levelheaded, so accustomed to looking out for his own best interests. And now in the past two days he, a penni-less, unemployed actor, had whistled a small fortune down the wind, not once but twice!

He could forgive himself the confession to Venetia. He had owed her that failed attempt to make amends. His eyes were tender as he recalled the feeling of her lips and the softness of her body that rainy day on the Paladian Bridge. But to tear up Wincanton's note! That was the height of folly. And why? All for a gesture. Just for the pleasure of watching that arrogant aristocrat for once in his life look disconcerted. He chuckled softly at the memory. Well, it had been worth something, at that. But not, by God, one thousand pounds. The chuckle ended in a curse.

Nicky had reached the Circus when Wincanton overtook him in his hired curricle. "Get in, Forbes. We have to talk."

And perhaps it was the discipline the army had instilled that caused Nicky to shrug and do so. Or perhaps he viewed the meeting as an opportunity to confess that on second thought he was now prepared to accept his share of the major's money. But the other didn't give Nicky time to sort this out. He flicked his reins and came right to the point.

"I think you'd best tell me why Venetia was crying be-fore you made your confession. That is, if it had anything to do with me."

Nicky saw no reason not to pour out the whole story. After all, there was a kind of inevitability about the situation. It was always the toff who got the girl.

At the conclusion of the narrative, the major seemed to mull the matter over. Then, "That was a damned decent thing you did, Forbes," he said. Even Nicholas, who had at least a glimmer, could not fully imagine just what it cost Wincanton to make that admission.

"Well, that's as may be," the actor answered. "The thing is, you're by no means out of the suds. Oh, Lady Venetia loves you right enough. But she's sorted out that you—not me—were the one that offered Amabel carte blanche. That didn't exactly send her into raptures, you know.

"By the by, I think you'd better let me out here," he said just before they came in sight of the Crescent. "I don't like the notion of us being seen together. Lady Stoke's been damned decent, but no sense rubbing salt in the wound, I'd say."

"I agree." Wincanton pulled up the horses. Then, just as Nicky was about to say he'd changed his mind about taking the blunt, Wincanton said, "I'll not insult you again, Forbes, by offering you money. But I do want you to know I think you've behaved well through all of this, and I must say I'm sorry for my part in the whole, shameful affair."

Nicky sighed inwardly for the lost fortune as he jumped down from the rig. "Consider it forgotten." He managed to sound magnanimous. "Oh, but there is one other thing, Wincanton." He reached for a horse's bridle just as the other started to flick the reins. "About my . . . *sister*. I want you to know that if you ever come sniffing around Amabel again, it'll be bellows to mend with you, and no mistake. And you can take that promissory note to *my* banker."

Wincanton haughtily stared back at him for a moment. Then, to both his own surprise and Nicky's amazement, his face relaxed into a grin. "I don't happen to think you could mill me down in a million years, Forbes. But maybe it's just as well you'll never get the chance to try. I wouldn't wish to risk discovering that you're the better man. For I'll admit now that I've underestimated you all along.

"As for Amabel—you've no cause to worry. I plan to

173

marry soon and be a good and faithful husband. So I doubt that you and I will be seeing each other again, which is just as well, given the mess we've made of things. But then perhaps it's a fitting punishment that we'll each always be just a little in love with the other's woman. Am I not right?'' He looked quizzically at Nicky, who refused to rise to the bait but reddened nonetheless. "Well, there it is, then. Anyhow—actor—I wish you luck.''

Wincanton cracked his whip, then turned his team in the road ,with a skill that brought a stab of envy to the other's breast. Nicky stood and watched as his erstwhile double dashed away down Lansdown Hill.

Wincanton champed at the bit for the next two hours, a time frame he'd arbitrarily chosen as sufficient for Nicholas to take leave of Lansdown Crescent. An inordinate amount of that time was spent upon the major's toilette. Perhaps it was the memory of the actor's bang-up-to-the-nines appearance that made him depart from his usual indifference to that sort of thing and discard five cravats before the waterfall arrangement that he strove for achieved perfection.

He arrived at Lady Stoke's front door, arrayed elegantly, if rather staidly (he regretted the bottle-green coat he'd given Forbes), in dark blue superfine and dove-gray trousers. When the butler opened the door in response to his knock, stared at him, and then looked puzzled, Wincanton was at a momentary loss as to how best to announce himself. Just as he'd feared, his "Major Wincanton to see Lady Venetia'' caused Hope's jaw to drop. After that, it required a foot placed swiftly in the door to prevent its being slammed shut right in his face.

"It's all right, Hope. You may admit the major.''

Lady Stoke, who'd been positioned at a window, had

anticipated this sort of contretemps and thus hurried from her chamber, though not quite in time to forestall it. Now she stood mid-stairway, surveying her true nephew. "Well, it's easy enough to see how the impersonation business came about. Although I do believe the other one's . . . a bit taller."

"Better-looking, I collect, was what you meant to say." Wincanton handed his tall black hat to the bemused butler and moved toward her. "How are you, Aunt Louisa?"

Her eyebrows broke all previous records for elevation. "Your concern for my health comes tardily, Nephew. So you will understand if I ain't too touched by it. In fact, I'll tell you straight out, if I had anything to say in the matter, you'd be cut from my late husband's will."

"I can't say I blame you." He glanced back at the butler, who seemed rooted. "Could we go somewhere and have a private word?"

"Several. We'll have 'em in my bedchamber. Hope, you can go inform Lady Venetia that the other Major Wincanton has come calling."

Lady Stoke glanced back over her shoulder as her nephew followed. "My word, you even limp! I must say that Win— Oh, for heaven's sake, I can never remember that boy's real name!"

"Nicholas Forbes. Though I'm certain," he added dryly, "you'd have called him 'Nicky.' "

She chuckled as she motioned him to a chair in her cheerful, cluttered chamber and chose one opposite it for herself. "The actor's got your nose out of joint, then, has he? Well, I don't wonder at it. You're going to have a prodigious lot to live up to. Now then," she commanded, "let's hear your version of this farce."

Lady Stoke nodded with satisfaction when he'd concluded. "Well, that's pretty well the same tale the other one told. With the same omissions, I daresay. Neither one of you has said just why you were so dead set on staying in London. Oh, I realize no one ever wants to visit relatives—especially in Bath—but to go to those lengths to avoid it? There was a female in it somewhere or I'm a Dutchman. But never mind that now. The question is, what do you intend to do about Venetia?''

"Marry her. If she'll have me.''

She nodded wisely. "But you ain't too sure she will, now, are you? Well, good enough for you, I'd say. It's high time one of you Wincantons learned to eat humble pie.'' She stood up. "But I won't keep you any longer. Her room's third on the left down this hall. And in spite of the shabby trick you played on me, I wish you well.'' She giggled suddenly. "Do you know, this has all been better than a play. I don't know when I've been so diverted.''

Wincanton walked over and kissed her on the cheek, astonishing himself for the second time that day. "You really are a sport, you know.''

"Well, now''—she beamed—"that's more like it. You may have picked up a thing or two from the actor at that. But don't dawdle here, lad, practicing charm on me. Get on with your wooing.'' She gave him a push toward the door.

"Oh, I almost forgot.'' Wincanton reached in his coat and drew out a sheaf of bank notes. "I meant to ask if you'd do me a favor, Aunt Louisa. Well, not for me so much as for the 'charming actor.' Could you see to it that Forbes gets the money he would have collected if he'd won the bet? He threw the blunt back in my face when I offered to pay him earlier. But I expect he's had second thoughts by now. So if you don't mind, just let him believe it's from you. That'll save his pride.''

Lady Stoke closed the bedchamber door rather noisily behind her nephew, counted a slow ten, then reopened it a tiny crack. Her ear was at that opening when Wincanton knocked on Lady Venetia's door. She heard a muffled "Who is it?" followed by a clearer "Go away! I don't wish to see you—ever," then winced for the destruction of her door as she heard a well-placed kick splinter the paneling. "Oh, well, it's a small price to pay to be rid of a companion," she told herself philosophically as she resumed her seat and picked up her neglected tambouring.

"Oh, it's you." Lady Venetia, reclining on a japanned couch, looked up with a stormy stare from the book she pretended to have been reading. "One never knows just whom the name Wincanton will produce. The only thing I am sure of is that I do not wish to see anyone of that name ever again. Now, will you please leave?"

He closed the damaged door to the extent of its capability and limped toward her. "No, I'll not go, Venetia, till I've said what I've come to say." He stood looking down at her, his heart in his eyes and misery etched upon his face. "I've never regretted anything so much as this deception I've been a party to. But despicable as that action was, if it causes me to lose you, all I can say is that the punishment far, far outweighs the crime. I love you, Venetia. I want to marry you. More than I've ever wanted anything in my entire life."

In spite of her hurt, her anger, her humiliation, his intensity was having its effect. But she was by no means ready to hoist the white flag of surrender yet. "Oh?" she answered coldly. "More than *anything*? Would that include two thousand pounds per annum and a house near Drury Lane? Those, I believe, are the terms of your arrangement with Miss Fawnhope."

"Oh, God," he groaned, and sat down on the couch at her feet. "I *have* no arrangement with Miss Fawnhope. Oh, I admit I made the offer. But that was before I met you, dammit. You're all I want. And I know now that you're all I ever wanted."

Lady Venetia was finding these words, coupled with his look of abject misery, immensely satisfactory. Still, she could not resist replying, "Your feelings do you credit, sir. Especially in light of the fact that Miss Fawnhope turned your offer down. Perhaps you are growing accustomed to rejection, Major Wincanton."

"The devil I am!" he retorted as he took her in his arms. "I'd better warn you now, Venetia. I've always gotten whatever I really wanted."

And as he kissed her hungrily, she faced the fact that in no way was she prepared to ruin his perfect record.

Chapter Nineteen

*I*t was time he broke the habit of behaving like a toff, Nicky Forbes told himself as he glumly watched the waiter set out the supper that he'd ordered. He could ill afford the gesture of a private parlor in the White Hart. But then, he'd had no choice if he hoped to see Amabel alone. She did not have the status of a private dressing room at the Theatre Royal, and the old dragon she roomed with was not about to let a male—brother or no—into her nunnery at this hour of the night. And so he'd brought her to the hotel to say their good-byes.

"Don't look so Friday-faced, Nicky dear," Amabel said as the door closed behind the waiter and she helped herself liberally to asparagus and prawns. "I'll settle up the bill."

He looked offended. "You'll do nothing of the kind. I asked you here."

"Come off it, Nicky. It's me, not Lady Venetia. So now, tell me. What's this all about?"

"Do I have to have a reason now to see you, Bella?"

Damn, but he was testy. Though why the devil he should be taking it out on her was beyond him. "No, look, I'm sorry. You're right. There is a reason I asked you here. I'm leaving Bath tomorrow morning." He glanced at the clock on the mantel. The hands had moved past midnight. "This morning, I should say. I just wanted to say good-bye, that's all."

"Oh, Nicky, so soon? I had thought you had till—" She put down her fork and stared in consternation. "Oh, no! You've lost the bet, haven't you? They've found you out. And it's my fault. I know it is. I never should have cornered Lady Venetia that way. But I had no way of knowing— Oh, Nicky, how much did you lose? I'll help you pay."

His eyes misted just a bit, and he looked at her gratefully. She really was a brick! "That's damned decent of you, Bella. But it ain't necessary. The swells called the wager off. Since Wincanton came haring down here and muddied the waters, they didn't think the thing was fair." He'd concluded it was prudent not to mention it was his confession to Venetia that had really undone him. And he certainly was not going to let her know that he'd thrown Wincanton's money back in his teeth. Lord, Bella would screech the White Hart down around his ears if she knew that.

"Well, that's certainly a relief." Amabel picked her fork back up and attacked a prawn. "At least you're no worse off than you were," she added philosophically.

No worse off than he was? Nicky mulled the words over

in his mind as he crumbled a roll to bits. He wished he could be quite sure of that.

Amabel watched him anxiously. "You didn't fall in love with Lady Venetia, did you, Nicky? I know you were betrothed, but I had thought it was to be just one of those marriage-of-convenience things. Oh, lord, Nicky, don't tell me your heart was engaged. I don't think I can bear it if you've been hurt by it all."

"No," he replied slowly, "I didn't fall in love with her. Oh, it wouldn't've been all that hard to do, you understand, but I didn't. Not as myself, at any rate. But there's something I have to tell you, Bella. Wincanton did. Fall in love with Lady Venetia, I mean. I am sorry."

He watched with horror as tears welled up into her eyes. "Oh, lord, Bella, I don't think I can bear it if *you've* been hurt by it all," he quoted as he handed one of Wincanton's fine linen handkerchiefs across the table.

She dabbed her eyes, streaking its snowy whiteness with leftover makeup, and gave Nicky a shaky smile. "We're really a pair, aren't we, Nicky dear?"

"Did you love him, Bella?" Why he kept asking that same question was beyond him. Perhaps he didn't believe the answers she'd made before.

"N-no. I don't suppose I ever really did. But oh, I wanted to marry him. I wanted it more than I've ever wanted anything in my life. I wanted to be a lady, Nicky. To live in a fine house. At a fine address. And be looked up to. That's what I wanted, Nicky. And Gareth could have given it to me. I wanted to be one of *them*."

"Did you, love?" He reached across the table and took her hand. "Well, I suppose the brotherly thing to do would be to say I'm sorry. But I ain't a bit of it. You see, I've had a taste of being one of them. And I won't say I didn't like a lot of it. Being waited on hand and foot, for instance. And being looked up to for nothing at all except for being wellborn. But when it comes right down to it, the business was beginning to get old. I was starting to get restless. I wanted to do something, not just be somebody, don't you know.''

''I know you're lying in your teeth''—she smiled—''but I guess I have to admire your attitude. So what is it you plan to do, Nicky darling?''

''Oh, go to Cheltenham. Try to get on there. And if that don't work out, then it's on to Bristol. At least there's one thing I've learned from all this, Bella.'' There was pride in his voice. ''And it's that I'm an actor. In spite of the nincompoop critics and Edmund Kean, I know it now. I played a marvelous toff, Bella. By George, I fooled the lot of 'em!''

''Bravo!'' She disengaged her hand to lift her wineglass in salute.

''And do you know what I really want to do, Bella?'' The words came tumbling out. ''I decided it all back there when I thought I actually was going to win that curst bet and would have the capital. God knows how long it will take me now, but I still mean to do it. I want to form my own company, Bella. Be an actor-manager. Shape my own destiny for a change, not be dependent on the whims of prima donnas like Kean—or on other managers. Besides''—he grinned—''I want to pocket the lion's share of the admission charges.''

Amabel's eyes were glowing. ''Oh, Nicky, how marvelous! Let's do it!''

''I beg your pardon?'' He stared blankly at her.

''I said, let's do it. Now. This very minute. Why, we'd have no trouble at all getting together a first-rate company. And with me for leading lady,'' she added modestly, "you'd pack the house every night. Oh, Nicky! Our own company! I'd like it above all things."

"I don't know what's in that wine you're drinking, Bella, but I'd like a little more of it." He poured a generous amount of champagne into his glass. "You must've missed a bit of what I've been telling you. I didn't win the wager."

"Oh, I heard all that." She airily waved his financial problems away. "I'm quite prepared, however, to back our little venture."

"You!" He looked scornful. "I know Drury Lane has paid you rather well. And maybe you'll pick up a nice piece of change for your work here. But what I'm talking about will take real capital."

She tossed her head. "I know that. And I'm good for it."

"The devil you say. Where did you get your hands on that kind of blunt?"

"From Lord Desmond Keating's father."

"Bella, you didn't!"

"Of course I didn't." She glared. "You, of all people, should know better. What I did do, however, was to accept a bribe. No need to tell me, Nicky"—she set her jaw stubbornly—"that it wasn't the thing to do."

Such a preachment had not occurred to him. "How much?" he asked.

"A thousand pounds if I'd break off with his precious son, which, if he had but known it, I'd planned to do for nothing. But then I decided that the old goat owed me something for ripping my character to shreds. Why, he spent the better part of an hour raving on about how I was dragging his heir to ruin! How I wasn't good enough to be their parlormaid, let alone marry into their family. Well, coming on the heels of Wincanton's carte blanche offer, it was the outside of enough. So I let the old behemoth pay up."

"Good for you, Bella," he crowed.

"Amabel," she corrected him automatically. "So you see, Nicky, you can start your company right away. With me as your partner."

Controlling partner, he thought wryly. Bella was a born bear leader, and with her putting up the blunt—

She seemed to read his mind. "Oh, I promise I'll leave the business end entirely up to you. But I do wish to have a say in the artistic management. What plays to do, the casting—that sort of thing."

"Done!" A huge grin split his handsome face. Well, what the hell. It might not have been the dream the way he'd dreamed it, but it did have this advantage over the original version: it kept Bella by his side.

"There is one thing, though." Her eyes were downcast, her voice so low he had to strain to hear it. "I am quite determined, in spite of recent disappointments, to marry. No offense, Nicky dear, but I do not wish to lead the kind of life your mother led."

"I see." He really didn't, actually, for in retrospect his mother struck him as the happiest-natured person he'd ever known. But then, Amabel was different, always had been. "You ain't still thinking of marrying a toff, are you? Seems to me you might be a lot happier with some rich mill owner. He wouldn't be half so condescending."

"I don't want a mill owner."

"Oh, well, then"—he shrugged—"it's your life, Bella."

"It's you I mean to marry."

His jaw collided with his shirt points. "Me!"

"Yes, you. I've done a lot of thinking, Nicky, and I've come to accept the fact that you're the only man I've ever truly loved or ever will. I had thought I could make do with Wincanton. He always did remind me of you, you know. But now I realize that it would never have done for me. It's you I want, Nicky. And I've been trying to think of a way I could have you and the kind of life I'd like to lead as well. And you've hit on it. Our company. We can make our own fortune. Oh, Nicky, dearest, don't look so stunned. It will be the very thing.''

By George, it could be, at that! Here he'd been lusting after Bella for donkey's years, but since she was so determined to marry above her station, the idea of their becoming leg-shackled had never occurred to him.

She watched his expression slowly change from dazed incredulity to a tenuous acceptance of the notion. ''Oh, Nicky, you goose!'' She jumped up and ran around the table to throw herself into his arms. His expression switched instantly to lecherous.

''Bella, you've got a vicious cruel streak in your nature,'' he protested some minutes later when she pulled away from him. ''No need to be so missish, love. We're betrothed, in case you've somehow forgotten.''

''I've not forgotten. And I don't intend to consummate my marriage here on the floor of the White Hart.''

''The couch, then?'' he asked hopefully.

''No, Nicky dearest.'' She was on her feet and tidying her hair before the convex glass that adorned the wall, and her eyes grew misty. ''Oh, Nicky, I've dreamed of a proper wedding, with a white lace dress, and flowers in my hair. I want to be married at St. Paul's. And I want the world to come. Do you mind all that too much, Nicky dear?''

He walked up behind her and wrapped her in his arms. The glass reflected the tender look he gave her and held it for a moment like a portrait enclosed by a gilt wood frame. ''No, I don't mind. We'll say our vows perched on the dome if that's what you want, Bella. For all I want is to be with you always and to try to make you happy.''

The words had no sooner left his mouth than he realized to his amazement that they were true.

Its passengers were about to board the London coach next morning when the clatter of hooves and the sound of a speeding carriage caused the heads in the queue to turn. '' 'Old up there, guv'nor!'' came a shout, and Nicky groaned as he recognized Lady Stoke's barouche with Jocko Hodges, dressed in spanking-new livery, holding the reins. "Hey, actor! I've a parcel for you. But you'd best come get it, for I can't leave me cattle.'' The tiger grinned impudently as his horses champed at their bits, impatient at being forced to stand stock-still again just as they'd hit their stride.

Nicky cursed under his breath but walked over to the equipage, Amabel trailing curiously behind.

The tiger's eyes grew wide at the sight of the gorgeous actress dressed in a modish mauve pelisse and bonnet. He whistled appreciatively. "You are the one for landing on your feet, I must say, guv.''

"You show a little respect for my fiancée.'' Nicky's expression evidently betrayed his impulse to jerk Jocko off the seat and shake him like a rag, for the tiger hastened to say, "No offense meant, guv. But lor', the lady's a treat to look at, and there's a fact.'' Amabel dimpled up at him, and his grin returned.

"You said you have something for me.'' Nicky spoke impatiently. "Well, then, what is it?''

"It's a parcel from me employer, Lady Stoke. Thought you'd be interested to know I've quit me old employer. His Major Wincanton performance fell short of yours, you see, guv. Too dull by half, he was.''

"What you mean is that he sacked you." Nicky caught the brown paper parcel Jocko tossed him.

"Our parting was by way of a mutual agreement," the other retorted. "I've no desire to return to Lunnon. I find more scope for me particular talents here in Bath. But that's all by the by. Anyhow, Lady Stoke says to tell you she misses you already and wishes you to have this parting gift. Be seeing you, guv. Ma'am." He tipped his hat saucily to Amabel, then sprang the horses.

"What an odd little man," she observed, but Nicky was too stunned to hear her. He was leafing through the packet of bank notes in his hand. "A thousand pounds," he breathed. "Louisa has sent me a thousand pounds!" His share of the bet! She'd actually made good his share of the bet! He broke into a radiant smile as it dawned upon him that he could now match Bella's capital in their new venture. She was a darling girl, of course, but it was just as well that they'd not begin their married life with her having the upper hand.

Amabel's eyes were big as cartwheels. "Lady Stoke made you a present of a thousand pounds?" she gasped as he retied the bundle and tucked it in his pocket. "Whatever for?" Her expression changed suddenly to outraged shock. "Nicholas! Surely not! That old lady! You wouldn't have! Or would you?"

"Hurry, Bella. They're about to leave." He took her hand and broke into a run.

But after he'd tossed her up onto the roof seat of the crowded coach and climbed up beside her, she reopened the subject. "Aren't you going to explain just why Lady Stoke sent you all that money?" she asked him.

"No, I don't think I am, Bella my love." He grinned. "For it wouldn't be at all the thing to my way of thinking. Not quite *gentlemunly*, you see."

FANCIFUL FREEDOM OF FORM EMPHASIZED THROUGH **IMAGINATION AND EMOTION**

Marian Devon